The Serpent's Children

Also by Laurence Yep

SWEETWATER

DRAGONWINGS

CHILD OF THE OWL

SEA GLASS

KIND HEARTS AND GENTLE MONSTERS

DRAGON OF THE LOST SEA

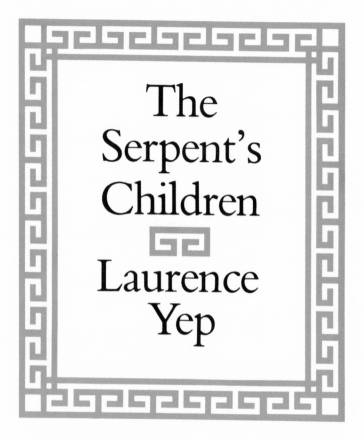

The
Serpent's
Children
Laurence
Yep

HARPER & ROW, PUBLISHERS

Library of Congress Cataloging in Publication Data
Yep, Laurence.
    The serpent's children.
    Summary: In nineteenth-century China, a young girl
struggles to protect her family from the threat of
bandits, famine, and an ideological conflict between her
father and brother.
    [1. China—History—19th century—Fiction.   2. Family
life—China—Fiction]   I. Title.
PZ7.Y44Sg   1984   [Fic]   82-48855
ISBN 0-06-026809-3
ISBN 0-06-026812-3 (lib. bdg.)

Designed by Al Cetta
1 2 3 4 5 6 7 8 9 10
First Edition

To Terry
and her daughters,
Franny, Lisa and Kathy,

to whom
I would entrust
any revolution.

```
☰☷
```

KU, the
eighteenth
trigram

from the
Book of Changes

"The superior person
rouses other people and
nourishes their hopes."

Chapter One

We had such high hopes when Father marched off to fight the demons. I was only eight at the time, so to me he seemed like a giant and his spear seemed to reach to the beams of the ceiling when I looked up at him.

"Are you sure you're going to be all right?" he asked Mother.

Mother was a small woman; but kilo for kilo she had more spirit than any of the men who would be marching with Father. She crinkled up her nose the way she did when she was happy, and she laughed at Father. "Of course—I'm fine. I just took some tonic for my cough. There's nothing quite like hairy mustard, you know."

Father nodded to the jars of herbs and flowers and other things she used in her cures. "You don't need more medicine. You just need rest. Maybe I should stay here and take care of the fields."

Mother patted Father on the chest. "I know you when something important is going on. You wouldn't do any more than stroke the weeds while you waited for news."

Early that spring, when we had begun planting the first rice crop, the village had been shocked to hear that the demons had invaded the Middle Kingdom—or *China*, as the demons called it. A fleet of ships, lean and sleek as hunting hounds, had appeared before the great city of Canton. And from the ships' holds had poured a horde of demons and their slaves. Demons weren't especially evil, since they could do good things for a person as well as bad. But these *British* demons wanted to force the government to let them sell their opium here.

The barbarian Manchus who ruled our country had seemed powerless to stop the demons. And though my parents did not love the Manchus, they loved the demons even less, so when the officials had asked the people for help, Father and Mother had decided he should go.

Father turned to my little brother, Foxfire, who was seven. Tapping a finger against Foxfire's nose, Father warned him, "Now I want you to be a regular little gallant and help your mother and big sister."

My little brother was a terrible crybaby. Mother said it was because he had a tender stomach that left him sick most of the time; but I thought he was a little monster who began crying the moment he didn't get his way. I was always having to give in to him.

There were times when I felt like pushing him down the nearest well. Mother and Father seemed willing to forgive Foxfire more because he was a boy. If I forgot one of my chores, I could expect a scolding. But Foxfire could dream all day, and nothing would happen to him. Our parents would laugh at his crazy notions, and tell me to do his tasks for him.

He was so much of a daydreamer, they'd nicknamed him Foxfire after the man in the story who went chasing after the glint of gold only to find it was the magical light made when foxes comb out their tails. My parents thought it was funny when he came up with such wild ideas. But they got annoyed with me if I didn't do exactly what I was told. I was supposed to be the practical one.

I looked contemptuously at my little brother as he started to bawl and back away from Father as if Father had suddenly grown horns and scales.

"Is it the spear?" Father asked anxiously. He leaned the spear against the wall and then held out his hands. "You see? It's just me."

But Foxfire continued to cry. It was times like those that I felt ashamed and angry and ready to slap him. But Father simply swept him up in his arms and swung him high in the air, and the bawling changed to little yips of excitement.

In the meantime, Mother had turned to the table to get Father his bundle of food. Suddenly she lurched forward against the table's edge and clapped a hand to her mouth. Her body shook as she tried to stifle her cough. Alarmed, I went over to her. "Mother?"

With her hand over her mouth, she shook her head at me not to say any more. She didn't want to Father to think he had to stay. I leaned against her with my hand on her back, feeling the spasms pass through her body—almost as if I were trying to draw the spasms out of her and into my own body by the magical touch of my hand. Father and Foxfire were still playing when the spasms ended and Mother lowered her hand.

She drew a shaky breath, testing her lungs, and then, with more confidence, drew another one. "We all have parts to play in the Work," she whispered to me.

As I said before, Mother may have been a small woman, but she was as tough and hard a fighter as Father. She had met Father through the Work—which was what they called the goal of driving out the Manchus and restoring the country to our people. And they had both carried out missions for the band of revolutionaries known as the Brotherhood.

She stretched out her hands for the bundle of food, but I was quicker, snatching the bundle and dragging it over so I could hug it to me. I didn't want her to waste any more of her energy. "Let me carry it."

Mother affectionately drew her thumb across my cheek. "That's my little trouper." With her hand on my shoulder, we went over to Father and my little brother. "Here," she said to Father. "We've put together a bundle of food for you."

Father's eyes widened when he saw the bundle. "But that's enough food for a campaign. You should take something out for yourself and the children."

"We can manage." Mother wagged her finger at Father. "Just drive the demons away."

"And then the Manchus," I chimed in.

Father set Foxfire back down and picked up his spear. He thumped the butt of his spear against the floor and planted his fist on his hip. "Banish the darkness," he said.

"Restore the light," Mother murmured. And then, after a pause, she added, "And come back to us soon."

Father dropped his fist and cradled his spear in the crook of his arm. "We've spent most of our lives working for a righteous kingdom, and yet we don't seem to be any closer to achieving it."

Mother smiled patiently. "No one said it was going to be easy." She put a hand on his arm and gave it a squeeze. "Maybe in some other life we'll have more peaceful times."

Father nodded at her lovingly. "I think Heaven owes us that much."

There was a knock at the door and Cousin Spider poked his head inside. "Hey, everyone's waiting to march." He was a thin-limbed young man in his thirties who seemed to be all arms and legs.

"You're in an awful hurry to be a hero." Father tied the bundle to the shaft of his spear.

Spider did a little dance in the doorway. "I'd like to get away before my father thinks up a new bunch of insults. I'm tired of hearing what a disgrace I am to the family name. I wish my father would forget that our family was rich back in my great-grandfather's day." Spider made a face. "We have five fields, and he calls it our 'estate.' "

Mother fetched a small round cake and handed it to Spider. He was the older of Uncle Windy's two sons, so more was expected of him. "Your father reminds me of a little rooster my family had once. It always felt like it had to act three times as big so the other animals wouldn't know how weak and helpless it really was."

Spider saluted her with the cake. "Well, it's no fun being on the pecking end."

Father took one last, loving look around our one-room house. He sometimes called it our meadow, because of all the clumps of herbs and wildflowers Mother had hanging from the beams of the ceiling. Then he pivoted and started for the doorway. "He'll change his tune when you come home a hero."

"I'll believe that when it happens." Spider backed away as Father approached.

Their fellow "warriors" were waiting in our court-yard. There were only six of them, but they filled the tiny space. Four of them were hardly more than boys, and they were armed only with hoes—as if the demons were so many weeds to be chopped.

But Spider bustled up to them. "Step into line. Try and look like heroes at least."

"There's plenty of time to practice marching on the way to Canton," Father scolded Spider. Then he squatted down to scoop up Foxfire in his free arm. I couldn't help feeling jealous. It was almost as if my brother had stolen my place; and though I resisted saying anything now, I couldn't help running to Father and clinging to his shirt.

"Cassia, behave yourself," Mother said sternly.

But that only made me tighten my grip. "No."

Father understood as he looked down at me. "Well, I think this other arm could use some exercise too." And with a laugh he handed the spear to Mother and then hoisted me up in his other arm. I gave a happy laugh as I went soaring into the air and Father jogged me up and down. "We'll do this for old time's sake."

"What a way to march into history." Spider shouldered his spear.

"We're fighting for the children," Father reminded him quietly.

And, with a child on either arm, Father led the way out of the courtyard. Everyone in the village belonged to the Young clan, so we were all related by marriage if not by blood. In a way, then, Father's little troop was the clan's army. Most of the clan were down in the fields working, so there were only children and old people in the dusty lane. But they called out good wishes to Father's little army. "Drive the demons into the sea," cheered one old lady.

"Give 'em a taste of good, cold steel," said another.

"But be careful." A bony little woman rushed forward and pressed a bundle into Spider's arms. It was Aunt Piety, Spider's mother. She must have snuck out of her house when her husband wasn't looking.

"I'll try." Spider reached out his hand to her, but his mother was already scurrying back toward their house. His hand groped only at empty air.

I couldn't have felt any prouder than I felt at that moment, as we paraded through the village with the sunlight all around us. It didn't seem as if anything could possibly stop Father and Spider. They were fighting for a cause that was just and good and against a terrible evil. I was sorry when he stopped by the village gates and set Foxfire down. Naturally, my little brother began to bawl again. And much to my shame and despite all my promises to myself, I could feel the tears begin to sting my eyes as well.

I clung to Father's neck for a moment. "Come back soon," I whispered.

"I will, child." Father gave me an extra squeeze before he put me down on my feet.

Mother held out his spear. "Remember. Don't try to hog all the glory at Canton. I'd rather have you march back through the door safe than hear tales about a dead hero."

Father touched her hand for a moment. "I think there'll be enough honor for all. We'll have our righteous kingdom yet." He took the spear from her and rested it on his shoulder. "And don't you be so proud that you try to do all the work yourself. Ask others for help."

"Oh, go on. I've been handling our fields well enough." Mother made a shooing motion with her hand as it he were some chicken that had strayed through the door.

Father's voice was husky as he beckoned his little army to follow him. "Well, come on. Canton isn't getting any closer by our standing here."

And they began to march down the path that zigzagged to the valley below. Though they tried to march in step, they didn't have any better luck than a flock of ducks waddling after one another. Heaven had to be on their side, so I didn't see how they could possibly fail.

Chapter Two

Father was no sooner out of sight than Mother lay down for a rest. I tried to keep Foxfire occupied by making little people out of straw; but he just wanted to whine.

"Why does Father have to fight for the Manchus? I thought he didn't like them."

I was still annoyed with him for crying, and I thought this was my chance to make him behave like a true warrior. I wagged a little straw man at him. "Don't be stupid. The demons are ten times worse than the Manchus."

I could see big tears welling up in his eyes and his lips beginning to quiver. "Don't call me names."

"Yes, you are stupid," I insisted, "and a crybaby too."

His mouth opened and shut several times as he tried to think of some response, but all he could manage was "I'm not a crybaby."

I stepped back in triumph. "There, you see. If Father could see you now, he'd be ashamed of you. He told you to be a gallant like him, and you can't even keep from crying the moment he's out of sight." Mother stirred on her mat of rice straw. I felt guilty for waking her up, and suddenly I wanted someone to blame. "And now you've woken up Mother."

That made Foxfire feel worse, so he began to cry even louder.

Mother stood over us, but she didn't scream or shout or slap us the way one of the other mothers would have done. She looked at us sadly—which made me feel as small and slimy as a snail. And I felt bad right then. "Mother, I'm sorry." I said.

She took my arm in one hand and Foxfire's arm in the other. "Hush, now," she said. "This is no way to behave."

Most of the time Mother was as serious as she could be; but there was an odd, whimsical streak that came out sometimes. And that was when she told the best stories.

Mother crinkled up her nose when she smiled. "You know this tale, but maybe you'd better hear it again. Come over to the story window." She led us over to a window lattice her father had carved. He had been a talented craftsman, and I could sit for hours tracing the intricate carvings on the wardrobe and chest my mother had brought with her. But the lattice was my special favorite.

Our grandfather had worked at the wood so cunningly that the light would slip through the lattice and cast the shadows of strange marshland monsters surrounding a serpent-woman. Our grandfather had been so skilled that more than once I'd found myself looking up, expecting to see that the shadows had been made by real creatures instead of by carvings.

As Mother sat down before her window, it was as if she were sinking among the shadows of her story. She sat me down next to her and took Foxfire onto her lap, and she told us about the young wanderer who went to look for work.

He wandered for many kilometers until he reached a village near the marshlands. But he had no sooner started to ask people for jobs when he heard a strange, lovely music coming from a tower by the edge of the marshes.

Sometimes it sounded like a deep-throated wind that spread itself thinner and thinner over the silvery waters and green reeds of the marsh—stretching outward until the wind itself was lost. And other times the music piped wild and free and hungry or warbled as happily as a bird or keened hollowly like a lost child.

One of the villagers saw he was listening to the music. She came over to warn him. "If you're smart, you won't listen to it. Otherwise she'll catch you in her spell."

"What do you mean?" the young man asked.

The village pointed toward a tower. "There's a snake-spirit that took over that tower a couple of years ago."

However, being curious, the wanderer ignored her warning. Drawn by the music, he left the village to see the snake-spirit for himself.

As he neared the tower, he was cautious enough to pick up a big stick to use as a club. And then, step by step, almost tiptoeing, he approached the tower door and swung it open.

There, sitting on the floor, was a young woman, pale and beautiful as the moon. And in her hands were the seventeen tubes of a hand-held reed organ.

She took the mouthpiece from her lips. "You'll find the jewelry over there," she said calmly, and pointed toward a chest beneath the stairs.

The wanderer had been expecting almost anything but a young woman. Ashamed, he threw the stick away. "I haven't come to rob you. I only wanted to see if there really was a serpent in the tower."

"I hate to disappoint you, but there's only myself." And she rose from the floor. Her pale, silver gown shimmered like the moonlight on the river, and her shoes and jewelry gleamed like the stars overhead.

"I'm not disappointed at all." The wanderer smiled. "But what are you doing here?"

The young woman told her sad tale. A cruel, greedy king had taken over her land and sent her into exile. She had traveled a long way before coming to the tower. Discovering that the nearby villagers thought it was haunted and were afraid to go near it, she had thought it would be a perfect refuge, and so she had ended her long journey.

The wanderer, already in love with her, believed her because he wanted to. So he busied himself about the tower, repairing things and making himself useful as he courted the young woman. And eventually she agreed to be his wife. As for the villagers, he told them there was no spirit in the tower. But since no one else wanted it, he would occupy it himself with his family.

No one made a fuss when he married the girl. They had a son soon and settled down to live happily ever after. But a priest came to their door one day to ask for alms for the Temple of the Golden Mountain.

The wife didn't want to have anything to do with the bald, ugly man. However, the wanderer, being bighearted, invited him inside. Miffed, the wife took their son up to their room upstairs.

Before very long before the young man was sorry that he hadn't listened to his wife; for the priest stared with a frown at everything—from the expensive rugs on the walls to the golden dishes and bowls. It was obvious that the priest disapproved of the place.

The wanderer was trying to think of some way to excuse himself when the priest insisted on seeing his hostess. Though the wanderer tried to stop him, the priest shoved past him. Angrily, the young man followed the priest upstairs into their bedroom. His wife sat in one corner of the room with their son in her arms.

"Why do you repay my kindness with such rudeness?" the wanderer demanded.

"On the contrary," the priest said. "I'm saving you." He pointed at the wife. "This is no woman. She's a snake-spirit who's tricked you."

"Stop him," the wife cried to her husband, but it was too late.

Drawing a magical symbol in the air, the priest said a quick spell and the enchantment was broken.

The elegant furnishings dissolved with a sigh into thin wisps of mist. And there, coiled around their son, lay a giant snake with soft, white scales that gleamed like old, polished ivory. She reared upward from her coils, and the man could see that her head was shaped not like the angular one of a snake but like the head of his wife.

With a cry of horror, the wanderer picked up their son and fled with the priest away from her and her tower.

The White Serpent lay for a long time on the floor. At first she was too surprised to do anything, but then she began to feel hurt. The hurt changed to anger. And once a serpent sets her mind on something, she doesn't give up—whether she's fighting a war or loving someone. She summoned a host of monsters from the marshlands. With her army behind her, she tracked her husband and her son to the very gates of the Temple of the Golden Mountain.

I looked at the corner of the window where my grandfather had carved a miniature temple as Mother began to describe the battle. The priests fought that magical army all that day until late in the evening, when the fighters collapsed in exhaustion. The wanderer sat beside the priest, both of them dozing beside the gates, when they heard the sound of a reed organ.

He peered through a small window in the gate and saw the White Serpent again in her human form. In her hand she held the musical instrument that he remembered so well.

"Don't listen," the priest warned him as he covered his own ears.

The wanderer tried to obey. He crouched down with his hands over his ears, but the music drew him. He began to remember all the good times they'd had together. Surely she hadn't been just amusing herself by fooling him. He was positive that she had loved him in her own way. But he had to know.

So, later that evening when the priest was asleep, the wanderer slipped through a side gate and went down to her. It was all he could do to keep himself from running back to the temple at the sight of all those strange, terrible beasts who growled and hissed at him. But the White Serpent stilled them with a single gesture of her hand.

He strode up to her. "Why did you trick me?" He meant to sound like a stern, angry warrior, but he couldn't keep the hurt from creeping into his voice.

She cradled the reed organ in her hands. "I have lived a long, long time. In fact, far longer than the rest of my kind. And over the years one becomes . . ." She shrugged in embarrassment. "One becomes lonely. And then one shape seems as good as another. I moved into the tower in the hopes of making friends with the villagers, but they were still frightened of me. Only you ever dared to come to me."

The wanderer thought about that for a long time before he spoke. "They say that when we die, we can be born again as a snake or a bird or a human or any other living creature," he reasoned. "So the shape of one particular life doesn't really matter, does it? In another life you might be the human and I might be the snake."

So the wanderer decided to accompany the Serpent back to her tower, but first he went to the monastery to reclaim their son.

The outraged priest glared at him. "You're the worst idiot I've ever met. You ought to know better than to let yourself be fooled a second time."

"It's the heart that counts," the wanderer said. And, carrying their son, he joined the White Serpent and they returned to the tower together.

The son grew up and married a woman from the village. And eventually one of his descendants left to found Mother's home village.

"So"—Mother tilted up her head—"you two mustn't fight, because you're of the same serpent blood. All you really have is one another."

"But we're all Youngs," I protested.

Mother shook her head. "You may have the clan name of Young, but you'll always be outsiders to them."

As Foxfire lay drowsily in Mother's lap, he looked just like an ugly little pig. It seemed hard to think that I was related to that thing, but I sighed. "If you say so."

Chapter Three

During the next two months, whenever I found myself getting mad at Foxfire, I would remind myself
of what Mother had said: Foxfire and I were kin,
after all. Anyway, the most important thing was that
Mother should rest and have peace and quiet. Late
one afternoon I took Foxfire out into our little courtyard to play while Mother napped.

Suddenly an impish head popped up above the
wall to our left. It was our neighbor, Aster. Though
she was twelve, we were good friends, and I think
we would have been good friends even if I hadn't

been the only girl who would talk to her.

Aster belonged to a group called Strangers. Around three hundred years ago when the Manchus had first conquered the Middle Kingdom, they had forced people to leave the coast so they couldn't help the troops loyal to the old emperor, who had taken over some islands. Some of those people had settled in our province where the name "Strangers" had been applied to them; and the name had stuck all this time.

Mother had gone out of her way to make friends with the Strangers when they had moved into the house to our left. As she had said, it seemed odd to call people "strangers" when they had been here so long. Maybe Aster's family wouldn't have seemed so strange if her people hadn't insisted on keeping their own language and traditions.

Aster had been betrothed to her husband, Tiny— also a Stranger—when they were both infants. She had come to stay with them just last year. Of course, she still lived more like a sister than a bride to Tiny, and would until they were both of a proper age. But that way Tiny's family would come to think of her as one of their own and she would avoid the trouble that a bride sometimes has with her in-laws.

She carefully set a bowl on top of the wall. "Here's some soup for your mother." She spoke in the clipped, monotonous way of the Strangers.

I climbed up on a bench and took the bowl. "Why don't you use the gates like everyone else?"

Her face became a mask of horror. "And have everyone know our business?"

I lowered the bowl and climbed down from the bench. "They hear us anyway."

Aster boosted herself up to the top of the wall and slung a leg over. "But they can't really be sure that we're serious without seeing our faces." She dropped down beside me.

"Who's that, dear?" Mother called from inside the house.

"It's Aster. She's brought some soup." The bowl itself was too hot to cradle against my stomach, so I held it before me as I stepped into our little one-room house.

Mother propped herself up on the mat. "Aster, thank your mother-in-law for me. She's really too kind."

"Oh, it's nothing." Aster paused in the doorway. "We just dragged the chicken through the water a couple more times."

Mother tried to laugh and wound up coughing.

[24]

I set the bowl down beside her. "Do you want some tea?"

"No, just a cup of hot water." Mother sniffed the steam rising from the bowl. "It smells wonderful."

"Thank you, ma'am. It's my mother-in-law's recipe." Aster stepped into the room and got a spoon for Mother. Aster had learned all the secrets of our home long ago.

"Well, tell your family we won't impose on them anymore." Mother sat all the way up. "I'm feeling much better now."

I put the water on to boil and then got a handful of dried weeds. "You were coughing all last night." I stepped around behind the brick stove and got a fire going in the hole beneath the stove.

"I was just clearing my lungs," Mother insisted, as much for Aster as for me.

"But we don't mind helping at all, ma'am," Aster said.

"It's almost time for the harvest. Your family will have to do its own fields," Mother said.

As soon as the fire was going, I walked around from behind the stove. "I still think you ought to rest a few more days."

Mother raised the bowl and dipped the spoon into the soup. "No, my mind's made up," she said in her sweet, firm voice. And I knew it didn't do any good to argue with her.

"Well, I'm going with you to the fields," I said then.

"Me too," Foxfire insisted.

Mother lifted the spoon and blew on the hot soup to cool it. "You're going to have to do what I say."

"Yessum," I said.

"And no quarreling." She looked at Foxfire and me.

"No, ma'am," I said.

"Well, you call us for the heavy work," Aster volunteered. "Don't make Cassia do everything. You don't want her to get muscles like a blacksmith." Her father-in-law had been a blacksmith until hard times had forced him to sell everything and turn to sharecropping. But little by little he was buying back his tools and teaching his son, Tiny, the trade.

Foxfire threw back his head and gave a laugh. "Then we could rent her out like a water buffalo so she could plow the fields."

"And I'll use you for a plow." I snatched at him, but he was already running out the doorway.

Mother sighed. "So much for promises."

"But that was for tomorrow." I drifted toward the

doorway so I could go after Foxfire. "And this is for today."

Mother nodded toward the stove. "The hot water" was all she said.

Of all the clan trudging down to the fields, only Mother would pause to watch the sunrise. And only Mother would make you feel that it was new. She stopped right in the middle of the path and turned her face to the east. "Oh, look at that sky. It's just like a piece of amber I saw once."

The sun was still hidden by the ridge top above our village, but its soft, golden light filled the world. She looked first at me and then at my little brother. "It's almost as if the light wasn't coming from the sun but from within us." Mother's face took on that excited look it did when she was caught up in some fantasy. "As if the light were streaming from each person and each thing. It's an inner light that shines through the cloth and bone and flesh, wood and hide and dirt."

When the sun topped the ridge the next moment, the light flowed through the trees and down the slope and over the village—sweeping the darkness from the rooftops as quickly as Mother swept her gateway. The sunlight went on, slipping down the sides of the valley to glide over the water in the rice fields so they shone like pieces of polished shell.

Walking with Mother was never simple. She liked people, and there was always someone who needed her help and advice. "I thought you were going to stay home and dose yourself with your medicines," Aunt Piety said.

Mother turned with her usual smile. "But I've got Foxfire and Cassia to help me." She winked affectionately, first at me and then at my little brother, who was smaller than the hoe he carried.

Aunt Piety tilted up the brim of her straw hat. "I know it's near harvesttime, and I know you have a lot of help today, but don't you think you ought to rest? I heard you were coughing up blood."

"I'll take it easy today," Mother said, and to change the subject, she took Aunt Piety's right hand, massaging the swollen knuckles. "Your hand seems better today."

Rheumatism made Aunt Piety's knuckles swell up and turn red. "Yes," she agreed. "I've been washing it in that solution you gave me, and the swelling's been going down faster than with anything I've ever used before."

Mother patted her hand. "It was my mother's herbal cure. She always said the roots from the peach of the drunken immortal work every time."

"This is no time to chat," said Uncle Windy. "You're blocking everyone." And he tried to shoo us away as if we were so many stray ducklings.

The clan itself was divided into three branches that traced their lineage back to the three sons of the First One. Though Uncle Windy wasn't the oldest in our branch, he made a point of trying to keep his unruly kin in line—especially my family. He looked at Mother at that moment as if he expected instant obedience.

But Mother just stood her ground, though Uncle was bearing down on her. "And how've you been eating, Uncle?"

"Well enough," Uncle Windy grumbled, "considering what your husband's done. He was crazy enough as a boy when he started calling himself 'the Gallant.' Then he had to bring you into the village and start breeding even crazier children. And then he had to go infect my older boy with his madness." He glared at Mother.

Mother's smile thinned a bit. "They're defending us and our land," she corrected Uncle.

"The only things those two fools will win are coffins—if they get even that much," Uncle Windy complained.

Aunt Piety frowned. "Don't talk like that in front of the children."

Uncle Windy seemed to notice us for the first time. "Well, it's time they faced up to the truth."

"Isn't Father coming back?" Foxfire piped up.

"Of course he is," I reassured my little brother. "After they've driven the demons into the sea."

"That's right," Mother said approvingly, "and then we'll get the Manchus and make *them* run." It always made me feel good when I did something Mother liked.

But Uncle Windy merely rolled his eyes heavenward. "Give me strength. It's bad enough I have to hear that nonsense in this generation, but do I have to hear it in the next as well?"

With a chuckle, Mother ushered us in front of her. "Come along, helpers." She called over her shoulder to Aunt Piety, "I've more of the solution if you need it."

Aunt Piety waved one hand to her. "I'll get some more tonight then."

When we reached the bottom of the path, we

joined the men and women of the clan walking along the dike tops that served as both borders and the paths of the fields. Like those of many of the other families in the clan, our "farm" was divided up into five little strips of land, each about a sixth of an acre, that were scattered all around the fringe areas of the valley where the farming was miserable.

Mother always headed for one special field first. Our father had once owned it, but hard times had forced him to sell it. We worked the land as share-croppers now, giving over a large portion of what we grew to the owner of the field, the Golden Cat.

To reach that field we had to pass by some of the prime fields, where the plants grew fat and healthy from the ridges of rich, black earth.

Foxfire paused to stare. "Why can't we grow plants like that?"

Mother started him moving again with a jerk at his hand. "Because the soil in our fields has more clay in it." She was trying to be patient as she explained, but her voice sounded strained. "And because these fields are easy to water and their owners can afford a lot more fertilizer than we can."

When we got to our field, I thought wistfully of the tall, healthy stalks. Our own plants were always such scraggly little things. "I wish we had a field like that. It's almost like we have to fight the dirt to let anything grow."

Mother rounded on her heel. "Don't you ever let me hear you talk that way again," she scolded me. "You've got an ancestor who died for this field."

I looked away from her toward the field as if there still might be traces of blood in the dirt. "Really!"

Mother seemed sorry she had lost her patience with me. When she spoke again, her voice was calmer. "It happened over two hundred years ago—when the Manchus were still trying to conquer our country. One of your ancestors tried to defend that field."

I could have understood if it was a prime field, but it was such a miserable little scrap of land. "But why?"

"Because it was his own." She leaned forward and pressed her face against mine urgently. "No, because it was *him*."

I scratched my forehead, puzzled. "What?"

"Don't you see, Cassia? *His* ancestors had already been working that same field for hundreds of years before him. Their blood and sweat went into the same soil. And the dirt grew the plants that went into their bodies—on and on in an endless cycle." She held out an arm toward us. "His flesh came from that dirt. So does yours. So hating the earth is like hating yourself."

"But what happened to him when he tried to defend the field?"

Mother sighed. "He met up with a Manchu horseman who was determined to take this one little patch of dirt from him. Your ancestor was cut down where he stood."

I picked up a handful of dirt from the dike and wondered which of my ancestors the dirt had once been part of. And for a strange moment, because of Mother's words, I could feel a kind of oneness with the field and the valley and the entire clan. It was as if the soil and our bodies were only different versions of each other. "Is that why you always come here first—so you can remember him?"

"That's part of it." Mother sat down on the dike and began to roll up her pants. "But I also like the view. It always makes me feel so . . . so fresh and new." The slope was steeper and rockier here, and it wasn't marked with terraced fields. The ridge was also lower, so the pine trees along the top were actually closer. Their green tops, still moist from the morning dew, seemed to sparkle and gleam like the helmets of tall sentries.

As I sat down beside her, it felt reassuring to think

of all the others of my family who had probably sat down in this very same spot to do the exact same thing. "Did that ancestor defend the field because of the view?"

"Maybe he even thought of it as his own." Mother started to lean over to help Foxfire roll up his trousers. But suddenly her whole body shook with a heavy, racking cough. I waited for it to pass, but the coughing went on and on. "Do you want me to get you some water?" I asked her.

She tried to shake her head, but the coughing became so bad that she slid off the dike into the field.

I jumped down from the dike into the field and saw that blood now flecked her lips.

"I'll go get her medicine." Foxfire turned, poised to run home.

Suddenly Mother pitched face forward into the muddy water.

I went to her and managed to raise her head. Her eyelids opened slowly as if they were now made of stone rather than flesh. "Take care of them," she said.

I brushed the mud from around her mouth. "Take care of who?"

"Your brother and father." Her words were barely more than a whisper, and I leaned forward to hear better. "Their minds are so busy walking in the clouds that their feet would trip over the first pebble if we weren't there to guide them."

"But you'll be there." I held Mother's wrist as if I could hold her souls within her body, but her pulse was already fluttering.

Mother managed a weak smile. "You're the strong one. Take care of them."

"You can't leave us now," I pleaded.

Mother seemed to be staring past me at something a great distance away. "Please," she murmured. "Please not yet. I still have so much to do."

I knew she was talking not to us but to the creatures who come for the spirits of the dead.

Foxfire was kneeling beside us and weeping. "You can't die. Not now."

But Mother's lips stilled and the look in her eyes grew more and more distant. Whatever had made her our mother was falling down a dark, cold well faster and faster. Her pulse tapped one last time and then it stopped.

I was frightened and angry all at the same time— as if Mother had abandoned us on purpose.

Aster stepped onto the dike to our right that separated her field from ours. "What's wrong?" she asked in a frightened voice.

[35]

I laid Mother's hand down against the earth. "Mother's dead."

Aunt Piety climbed over the dike to our left. "Oh, you poor, poor things." She high-stepped among the rice plants until she could squat down beside Mother and try to feel her pulse.

Uncle Windy climbed up on top of the dike. "Well, old woman?"

"She's dead." Aunt Piety sighed and closed Mother's eyes.

Uncle Windy had rubbed an exasperated hand down his cheek and he nodded to us. "And their father's probably already gotten himself killed."

"No" was all I could say.

Uncle Windy had slapped his hands helplessly against his sides. "Well, how are we going to find him? It's like looking for a leaf in a windstorm." He looked at us as if we were two useless ducklings with broken beaks. "What are we ever going to do with you?"

I remembered what Mother had told me to do, so I looked up at Uncle Windy defiantly. "We can take care of ourselves."

Uncle Windy only snorted skeptically. "I'm hardly going to take your word for it, brat."

"I'll see to them," Aster said loyally.

Uncle Windy looked at her even more skeptically. "You're hardly more than a child yourself."

"You grow up fast around here." Aster stepped down into the field and started toward us.

Aunt Piety motioned her to stay away. "Now, now, never let it be said that the clan doesn't take care of its own." She reached out a hand toward me. "Come along, children. You can stay with us."

"Why should we—" Uncle Windy began indignantly.

But Aunt Piety wagged her finger at him. "And not another word out of you, old man."

And the other clan members who were beginning to gather to watch the spectacle laughed to one another.

But I didn't want to live with Uncle Windy. "No, we have a home."

"Now, don't be scared of your Uncle Windy." Aunt Piety took my wrist and tried to pull me away from Aster and Foxfire.

I'm sorry to say that I did the first thing that came into my head. I bit poor Aunt Piety as hard as I could. She let out a shrill yell, and still I clung to her hand.

Aunt Piety shoved me away and retreated several steps, rubbing her wounded hand.

[37]

The Golden Cat, the richest man in the clan, had been attracted by the crowd. He stared down at me now. "It seems," he observed, "that the little viper has her fangs already."

For the time being at least, the clan left us alone. Some of the men stepped down into our field and, keeping a wary eye on me, picked up our mother's corpse and carried her back to our little one-room house.

I remembered what Mother had said about taking care of my little brother. He looked so small and helpless at that moment that I hugged him tightly. "It's going to be all right," I said. "I'll always be here to protect you."

We rocked back and forth together until the tears stopped.

Chapter Four

—

I don't remember much about the funeral—except that there was wailing and other noises. But when it was over, Uncle Windy planted a fist on either hip and stared down at me solemnly. "You and I," he informed me, "are going to get along well. Do you understand me, child?"

"The child understands, don't you?" Aunt Piety put her hand over my hair. "She's going to be the little girl I never had."

But I shied away from her. "I don't see why we can't live in our old house," I complained.

"Because you can't expect your aunt to go running back and forth between the houses." Uncle Windy cupped my chin in his hand and tilted my head far back. "And anyway, it's time we trimmed your rough edges to bring out your beauty."

Holding on to my pigtails, I backed away from him. "You're not going to trim my hair," I said.

"No"—he smiled secretively—"not your hair. But what I have in mind will help us marry you off easily when the time comes."

I was puzzled by that, but Uncle wouldn't say anything more.

Aunt Piety left early the next morning, returning in the afternoon with an elderly woman who had long silver hairs growing from a mole on her throat. I recognized her as the matchmaker from town who arranged marriages and such things.

With them was a woman in her thirties riding in a sedan chair. As soon as she stepped out, the bearers set it down and I saw why she had to be carried.

I doubted if either foot could have been more than ten centimeters long. Each was encased in an embroidered slipper with a kind of high heel—but in the very center of the sole. Both Foxfire and I stopped playing to stare.

"Foxfire, dear," Aunt Piety said in her sweetest voice, "run along and play."

"No." Foxfire looked stubborn. Since Mother had died, he hadn't left my side.

Though Aunt Piety kept on smiling, her voice took on a sharper edge. "Go and play. This is going to be female talk."

"It's all right," I whispered in his ear. "It won't take long."

Reluctantly, Foxfire took a step away from me. I nodded to him encouragingly and he shuffled out into the lane.

"I'd like to sit down if I could," the young woman said, looking around.

"Please, inside." Aunt Piety bowed them both into her house.

Despite her handicap, the young woman managed to totter on her own into Uncle Windy's house. She sat down immediately on the nearest bench.

"You know Aunt Patience," Aunt Piety said to me, "and this is her niece, Lily."

"I'll get you some tea," I said politely, but Aunt Patience grasped my arm. "Such a pretty little thing."

"She's as brown as a buffalo, though," Lily commented.

"But the color's there," Aunt Patience defended me. "Good, high color." She stroked my cheek with one gnarled finger. "It shows spirit."

"Thank you. May I go now?" There was something about the way that Aunt Patience was scrutinizing me that made me feel uncomfortable.

"Not yet, dear." Aunt Piety took the matchmaker by one arm and me by the other and led us over to the same bench on which Lily was sitting. "She's a good girl."

Aunt Patience plopped down on the bench. "Then I'll make a fine match for you someday. We'll marry you to a rich man like my Lily here."

I frowned. "I don't want a rich husband."

Lily looked at me as if I had lost my senses. "But you can sit around all day letting the servants do everything for you."

"Do you see my foot?" Aunt Patience crossed her right leg over her left knee and took off her shoe so that I could see the wide foot with its splayed, callused toes. "It's as ugly as the roots of a tree. That's because I never had the opportunity to have it properly taken care of."

"It looks normal," I said.

"It's as ugly as a man's foot," Aunt Patience corrected me. "But you could have pretty feet—like Lily's." And she jerked her head at her niece.

Lily crossed her legs so she could slip off a slipper—a tiny thing no longer than a woman's index finger. Now that she was holding the slipper in her hand, I could see it was a small thing with delicate embroidery.

Lily held out her foot, which was bound in wide ribbons of blue silk. "There, do you see how lovely it is?" she asked proudly. Despite the heavy amounts of perfume, I could smell the sweaty, unwashed flesh.

Aunt Patience's palms cupped Lily's foot. "It's shaped just like a lotus blossom, delicate and perfect."

I stepped back, horrified. "No, it looks like a hoof."

"What are you saying, child?" Aunt Patience said indignantly. "Every man will turn to stare at you as you walk by on feet as dainty as Lily's." Aunt Patience nodded her head toward me. "It's you and I who walk like buffalo, not like real women."

But I couldn't take my eyes or mind off Lily's deformed feet. I'd heard that the Golden Cat's wife had bound feet, but since she didn't stir from their big house, I'd never seen them.

"Where are your toes?" I wanted to know.

Lily pointed toward the sole of her foot. "They've been gradually bent underneath."

"Didn't that hurt?" I wondered.

[43]

Lily shrugged. "Awhile." She added slyly, "But I hardly had to do anything at all. I just sat around all day eating and sleeping." She slipped her foot back into her tiny shoe. "My feet were shaped the way a tree or a shrub is formed in a garden to bring out its beauty."

I still found it hard to believe that my uncle and aunt intended Lily's fate for me. "But I want to be able to go for long walks and to run," I shouted. Aunt Patience grabbed my wrist.

"We know what's best for you, dear." She dragged me toward her.

"Watch her teeth," Aunt Piety warned.

"I think we'd better begin," Aunt Patience panted to Aunt Piety. "Once it's started, she won't have much choice. Get the sack from the sedan chair."

Aunt Piety looked at me helplessly. "Really, dear, you'll thank us later." And she called outside to one of the bearers of the sedan chair to bring in the sack.

For an old woman, Aunt Patience had a remarkably strong grip. "We'll do this gradually," she explained in a gentle voice. "A little bit at time, you see, to let the bones grow downward and then under."

While one of the bearers held me against the bench,

[44]

Aunt Patience took meters of bandages from the sack. "You can't do this. Father would never allow it," I protested to her.

"It's time someone helped you face facts, child. Even if your father is alive—which he probably isn't— he would still have a hard time marrying you off without a dowry."

"No." I twisted in shock and outrage. It didn't seem to be my toes that Aunt Patience slowly began to curl down, my foot she began to bind with Lily's help.

At first it was only a vague discomfort, but as Aunt Patience began to bind my other foot, the first one began to ache. And the pain suddenly made me aware that it was my feet being bound. "It hurts," I yelled.

Aunt Patience stroked my arm. "Of course it does, dear; but only a little bit at a time."

As the ache began to grow, I winced. "For how long?"

"A year. Maybe two." Lily kept on winding the bandages around my second foot.

"A year?" My toes ached right now as if they were in a shoe several sizes too small. I could not imagine what the pain would be like once the toes were bent

[45]

underneath the sole of my foot. "And what if I want them to grow back like they were?"

"They won't, dear." Lily finished tying the bandages with a large bow. "They'll go on staying beautiful."

"And hurting, is that it?"

Aunt Piety patted my foot. "Not as long as you keep them bound."

I stared down at Lily's feet. "You mean you can't even wash them?"

"Yes, you can; but it hurts," Lily said matter-of-factly. "So you only do it once in a while."

I stared at her. "Is that why your feet stink?"

"Really." Lily stiffened.

Aunt Patience shook her finger at me. "Her husband buys the finest perfumes for her feet."

"Yes, buys it by the jug. And that cheap scent still doesn't work." The chair bearer had relaxed his grip slightly because I hadn't tried to do anything up till now. So it was easy to pull free.

"No, you'll get the bandages dirty." Aunt Patience made a grab for me.

I took two tottering steps toward the door and felt the pain knifing up my calves and through my legs. I couldn't get my balance, and I found myself falling.

"You can't do this to me!" When I fell down, I began to scramble on my hands and knees into the courtyard.

"Now, dear, it will be all right." Aunt Patience tried to block my way.

I let out one shrill scream of horror and frustration and scratched, kicked, hit and bit her. And I can't describe the satisfaction I felt when I heard the matchmaker shriek.

"You willful, ungrateful, spiteful child." Aunt Piety began slapping me across the head and shoulders, but I kept on fighting the matchmaker.

It must have been quite a spectacle for the clan. They came running up to the gates to Uncle Windy's courtyard.

I looked at the bearers and then toward the street. But I didn't see Aster. However, a lot of the clan were there, and I held out a hand to my kin. "Help! They're trying to cripple me."

"How dare you. H-o-w dare you!" Aunt Luckless strode into the courtyard. I thought she meant to hit the matchmaker, but it was me she punched. "Let go of that poor woman. You ought to be grateful that your uncle and aunt are willing to go to all this trouble for you."

[47]

It was like a plot among the grown-ups, so I looked instead toward the children. One of them was a cousin by the name of Peony. She was a small, sweet-tempered girl about my age who lived two houses down from ours. "Help me."

Peony drew her eyebrows together, puzzled. "Why? I mean, I wish I could bind my feet. Then I'd only have to do light housework."

Aunt Luckless and Aunt Piety managed to drag me away from the matchmaker. As I struggled between them, I appealed to Peony. "But it hurts. It hurts real bad."

Peony tried to smile at me encouragingly. "But the pain goes away after a while, and then you're set for life. You'll be able to get a rich husband." And though the other girls didn't look quite as enthusiastic, they nodded their heads in agreement.

"And in the meantime," one of the other girls said, "they can't expect you to do any heavy chores."

"I wish I could trade places with you," Peony added.

I simply stared at the rest of the clan. They looked as dumb as water buffalo—big, hideous buffalo. And for the first time I truly felt alone. Our bodies might come from the same soil, but our minds did not. I

[48]

might as well have begged for help from clods of dirt.

And suddenly Foxfire came flying into the courtyard. "What are you doing to my sister?"

Aunt Piety caught him by the stomach before he could fling himself onto the matchmaker. "Don't be stupid like your sister."

But Foxfire flailed at her with his fists. "Let go of her. Let go."

And even as I went on fighting to get free, I was sorry that I had thought anything bad about Foxfire, or ever been jealous of him. Mother had been right after all: We were of the same blood. "Don't hurt my brother," I warned them. And I meant it.

But the bearers had swooped down at me and carried me back inside the house like butchers bringing a pig to the slaughter.

"Mother," I screamed. "Mother." The words just came out of some raw hurt inside me though I knew it wouldn't do any good. Mother was dead and could never hear me.

Chapter Five

I lay for a long time that night listening to the matchmaker snore. She was supposed to keep me from
undoing the bandages, but she'd had so much wine
with her supper that she'd fallen into a deep sleep.

I thought about running away to find Father, but
Canton seemed so very far away. And besides, I
didn't want to go away from Three Willows. This
was my home. This was where my ancestors had
lived and died. And so had Mother. Leaving the
valley now would have been like deserting them and
everything they had fought for. No, I couldn't go.
I would stay and fight for what was mine.

I sat up cautiously, but the matchmaker didn't

stir. Hardly daring to breathe for fear of waking her, I untied the bandages, unwinding them slowly from around my feet until they made two piles. Then I limped outside to where Foxfire slept on the floor.

Looking at my little brother, I felt guilty for thinking all those mean things about him. Of all the people in the clan, he had been the only one to try to come to my rescue.

When I touched his shoulder, his eyelids rose sleepily. "Come on," I whispered to him. "We're going home. I don't want to stay another moment under this roof." I helped him to his feet; then I took his hand, and we made our way out of the house and across the courtyard.

The bar had been set across the gates. We pushed and tugged it off and set it down on the ground.

Opening one gate cautiously, I peered out. Everything was quiet. "Let's go." Grabbing his hand again, I pulled him into the narrow lane.

He looked down at my feet. "Do they hurt?"

"A little, but they're getting better." I shuffled across the lane to our house. I half expected to hear the matchmaker begin shouting and raising the alarm, but there wasn't a sound from Uncle Windy's house. Still, I didn't relax until we were inside our own courtyard and the gates were barred.

[51]

Then I opened the front door to our little one-room house. Even though it was dark, I knew we were home because there were the familiar smells of all of Mother's herbs. I could see some of them in the light from the doorway as they hung from the rafters. Dried mugwort, and the little flowers of honeysuckle, and hog fennel that was so good for coughs.

Mother should be boiling one of her concoctions at the stove and humming to herself, I thought. And it hurt when I realized that she never would.

"Wait. I'll put up the shutter." Foxfire ran outside to prop the shutter up above the window. I kept my back turned until the moonlight fell through the window lattice. And then, despite the ache in my feet, I pivoted slowly so I could face the story window. And the familiar shadows seemed to writhe and curl across the floor to gather about my feet. I knelt down, feeling reassured by the shadows from the window. As long as they were there, I felt as if Mother would come through the door at any moment and begin one of her stories.

"I'm sleepy, Cassia," Foxfire yawned from the doorway.

I smiled at him and patted my leg. "Then come and put your head on my lap."

"I wish Mother was here," Foxfire murmured.

"I know, but this lap will have to do." I beckoned to him.

Shutting the door, Foxfire crossed the room and lay down beside me, resting his head on my leg. His tears felt hot and wet. "I just feel so alone." He bit out the words as if they hurt him.

And inside me, I could feel the same kind of ache. "I know. I know." I ran my hand soothingly over his head. "So do I."

He looked so small and fragile at that moment that I just wanted to protect him. And I felt almost if my heart were the wick of an oil lamp and someone had suddenly lit it. I stroked his head, crooning one of my mother's tunes in a low voice until he began his little baby snores. I couldn't have felt closer to him if he'd been my own child. "Nothing bad is ever going to happen to you," I murmured.

And I wondered what the White Serpent would have done at a time like this. In the first place, she would never have let fools take her away from her home. And she certainly would never have let them try to cripple her. It was time that I started to act like one of her children and fight.

Foxfire stirred, flinging out an arm. And I knew I had to fight not just for myself but for him as well.

[53]

I began to croon to him softly again, and he grew still once more.

I was ready for Uncle Windy when he came for me the next morning. He rattled at the gates and then banged at them. "Open up. I'm going to give you the switching of your life."

I raised the bamboo pole above the wall so that he could see the kitchen knife that was tied to it. "I'll stick you like a pig," I warned him.

"I think she means it," Aunt Piety said anxiously to her husband. I could hear the voices of the other neighbors gathering in the lane.

"She's only eight," our cousin Harmony said. He was Peony's father.

"But her father's taught her some of the martial arts," Uncle Windy said cautiously.

"They're just drills—exercises for a child." Harmony tried to encourage him.

"Then you're welcome to climb over the wall and take it away from her," Aunt Piety said.

Harmony, however, was less courageous when his own life was involved. "She might get lucky."

I could just make out Uncle Windy's eye peering through the crack between the two gates. "You're an ungrateful, wicked little child," he shouted at me. "We're only trying to do what's right for you."

"Leave me alone." And I thrust my homemade spear at the gates so that the tip of the blade slipped between them.

Uncle Windy's eye disappeared immediately. "She's lost her senses completely."

"It's the serpent's blood coming out in her," Aunt Luckless declared. "I knew bringing her mother into this village would bring no good."

"Nonsense," Aunt Piety tried to defend me. "She's just high-spirited. And her mother was a good woman."

"And I tell you it's the serpent's blood. They're cold-blooded, deceitful things," Aunt Luckless said with firm conviction. "You're better off letting them starve and making an end of this whole affair."

When my uncle and aunt began to whisper to one another anxiously, I took a step closer to the gates to try to overhear them.

"Just give them a little time," my aunt was whispering. "They'll come back to us when they're hungry."

"But we have to stop her from acting so crazy," my uncle protested. "We have to stop these rumors about snake's blood right now. They belong to our branch of the clan, after all."

"Fine," my aunt snapped. "Then you go in after her."

I stepped back, tightening my grip on my spear. Small feet crossed the dirt of the courtyard, and I glanced behind me to see that Foxfire had come out. He was dragging a hoe behind him.

"Why didn't you wake me, Cassia?" he scolded me. "I wanted to help."

I looked at him gratefully. Nothing, I told myself, was ever going to come between us again. "I'll remember the next time," I promised, and turned back to watch for signs of trouble.

There was a thump as Uncle Windy's body hit the wall and his hands clutched at the top. His head poked just over the top as he started to pull himself up.

"I warned you," I yelled, and lunged at him just as Father had taught me.

With a yelp, Uncle Windy disappeared before the point of the spear ever got near him. There were some thuds and angry shouts as he landed on top of several spectators.

Foxfire giggled behind me. It was catching. Though

I had meant to be a stern-faced warrior, I couldn't help chuckling.

When Uncle Windy had pulled himself together, he raised his voice shrilly. "You can starve for all I care. I wash my hands of you, you hear?"

"It's about time," I yelled back defiantly.

I could hear the neighbors buzzing to one another about us and our ancestry. I turned back to Foxfire.

He squared his shoulders proudly. "I guess we showed them."

Suddenly I was afraid, because I wasn't sure if I had done the right thing. I had promised Mother that I would take care of Foxfire.

"I think Uncle Windy would take *you* back," I warned him. "You're a boy, so you'd be safe. They wouldn't try to bind your feet."

Foxfire screwed up his face as if I had just pinched him. "You're all that I have left."

"Meals aren't going to be much. I just know how to boil rice."

"I don't care," he said.

"And it's going to be hard in the fields," I added. "You'll have to do what I say and not complain."

He hesitated but then gave in with a shrug. "Someone has to be boss."

[57]

"You're awfully agreeable," I said, a bit surprised.

"You're not much," he said, "but you are my sister, after all."

I felt warm inside right then. Maybe things would be all right after all. Mother's body might be dead, but her spirit certainly was still with us.

Chapter Six

Uncle Windy was waiting for us outside the gates later that morning. I set down the manure bucket and put my hand to the hilt of the kitchen knife from the ragged sash tied around my waist. And Foxfire got the stick he'd tucked through his waistband.

People in the lane paused to stare at us, and I saw one or two of them even make a sign against evil. Aunt Luckless's spiteful words had found a few believers. Even so, both of us felt more than a match for Uncle Windy or any other grown-ups who thought they could boss us around.

However, Uncle Windy just held up his hands. "I don't want a war. But how do the two of you

[59]

ever expect to harvest your rice? A threshing box is too big for two little bitty things like you."

"They won't have to," a voice piped up. And we saw Aster making her way over to us with her two tall brothers-in-law behind her. "They still have some friends here."

"You stay out of this," Uncle Windy warned her. "The clan can take care of its own."

"You're doing a mighty poor job of it," Aster snapped.

"You watch your tongue, girl, or—" Uncle Windy started to raise his hand menacingly.

"Or what?" One of Aster's tall brothers-in-law stepped up next to her.

Uncle Windy swallowed and lowered his hand. "Or she might waggle that tongue off."

"That's our problem, don't you think?" The Stranger beckoned to his brother, and together they picked up the manure bucket for us.

I bit my lip anxiously. At best, the clan barely tolerated the Strangers, so I was afraid for them. "Don't get into trouble on our account. We can manage."

"I'm sure you can," the first said with a reassuring grin. "But let us repay some of your mother's kindnesses to us."

"She cured my foot when those worms got into it," the second reminded me.

"And I've lost count of all the colds she cured in our family," the first one added.

"Well"—I stepped back—"for my mother's sake then."

Uncle Windy waved his hand in disgust at the Strangers. "You'll be sorry that you took up with the likes of them." He stomped angrily back to his house.

Aster hooked her arm with mine. "I went to get my family as soon as I heard you were loose."

I patted her hand. "And not a moment too soon."

With the help of Aster's family, we managed to harvest our first rice crop and plant the second. Foxfire and I settled back into a steady routine of work— as if Mother had never died. The work helped distract us from our grief and fear.

Two weeks later I was woken up one evening by shouting. I grabbed hold of the knife and got up. I thought it might be Uncle Windy or some other snoopy member of the clan trying to help us whether we wanted it or not.

But then, as I shuffled toward the door, I heard a woman wailing, and then a man joined in. And then other men and women. It was even worse than

Mother's funeral—as if the world itself were coming to an end. Fear sent a prickling sensation along my spine and into my stomach—as if thousands of little hairs had suddenly sprouted on my insides.

"Hurry, let us in," someone was shouting outside our gates.

I jerked the door open. "Who . . . who is it?"

"It's me, Spider. I've got your father. He's been hurt."

Dropping the knife, I ran to the gates and shoved the bar back. Spider and Father both had beards, and their hair was long and shaggy. Their clothes were dirty and tattered. Around Father's leg was a big, bloody bandage. And beyond them I could see people crying in the lane.

But for the moment, all I could think of was that I'd been right. "Father, you're alive." I threw my arms around him.

"Oof." He laughed. "Don't squeeze the breath out of me like that. I'm not too steady on my feet."

"What happened to you?" I asked.

Leaning on Spider, Father limped into the courtyard. "We were whipping the demons at Three Powers village when I took a lead ball in my leg."

"But we beat them anyway," Spider boasted. "We chased them all over the countryside."

"So we won the war?" The look on Spider's face made me stop.

"No, the merchants and the officials betrayed us. They wanted profits and bribes, not victories, so they made a peace treaty with the demons." He clenched one fist in the air. "Just when we had victory right in our hands."

Suddenly I understood the wailing outside, which was growing in volume as more and more people heard the news.

Father sighed as if it were an old argument between Spider and himself. "We won at Three Powers, but we lost every other battle. We would have lost the war anyway. Their weapons were terrifying." Father shook his head. "They know how to kill people so quickly and so efficiently."

"But they don't have good hearts," Spider said sternly. "And that will be their downfall eventually."

"A good heart doesn't stop a bullet." Father held on to the doorway and peered inside. "We'd better be prepared for the next war." He craned his neck as if he were trying to see into the darkened house. "Where's Mother?"

It was a moment before I found my voice. "She's dead, Father."

Father just stood in the doorway, but his knuckles turned white as he gripped the wood tighter. "How did it happen? When?"

"You know how long she had that cough." I put my hand on his arm. "It just got worse and worse. She died shortly after you left."

Father's shoulders sagged. "I knew I shouldn't have gone. If I'd stayed, I could have made her rest and get her strength back."

"But she told you to go," Spider argued. "She was as dedicated to saving this country as any of us."

"And now I won't be able to carry on the Work anyway," Father muttered. "It was all so useless."

"The leg will heal." Spider tried to encourage him.

Father bent even lower, as if he were suddenly trying to bear a great weight. "You heard the surgeon. He said that I'd always have a limp. And you need two good legs to perform a mission. But I wouldn't care, if Cassia's mother were still here."

I knew what it meant for Father to lose the Work and Mother at the same time. "There are things you can do for the Work here," I said to Father.

"Yes." Spider eagerly expanded. "You've always talked about training the militia so that it's like a real fighting force."

Father straightened ever so slightly. "That's true."

"And you can talk to people about the Work," I added.

"You're still needed." Spider put his hand underneath Father's left elbow.

"What happened to the others?" I asked as I took Father's right elbow.

"One died of dysentery, but the others made it home." Father limped slowly inside.

Foxfire sat up on his mat, rubbing his eyes sleepily. "Father? What's wrong with your leg?"

"A wound's thrown my stride off a bit." Father lowered himself onto a bench by the table and thrust his wounded leg out stiffly.

"Maybe Mother has something to cure it." Foxfire twisted his head around to look at the shelves on the wall.

Father surveyed the many jars. "I don't think there's anything there that will let me grow a new leg, though."

Foxfire sat down beside Father. "They tried to bind Cassia's feet, but we fought them."

Father drew his eyebrows together angrily. "Who did that to you?"

"Uncle Windy," Foxfire said.

Spider's head snapped up straight. "I knew how pigheaded my father was. But I didn't think he was that stupid." Spider spun around and ran for the door.

Father tried to rise and snatch at Spider's shirt, but he was too late. Frustrated, he sat back down. "Spider," he shouted, "don't go over there while you're angry. She's all right, after all."

But Spider was already racing across the courtyard and out the gates. Father slapped the thigh of his wounded leg as if it were to blame for all our troubles. "That fool is just going to make more trouble." He pointed to a corner. "Better get out a spare mat. I think your Cousin Spider is going to be sleeping here tonight."

I was serving tea to Father when Spider returned. "Well, it's over." He slouched against the doorway.

"What's over?" Father motioned me to take the cup of tea over to my cousin.

"My father's kicked me out. He's tired of having me disgrace our 'great house.' " Spider took the cup from me with a nod of thanks. "So he's disowned me."

"Let me talk to him." Father grabbed hold of the table and tried to shove himself to his feet. But Spider waved him back down.

"It was coming one day. If not over this, then over something else." Spider sipped his tea.

Father motioned to the mat. "Sleep here tonight

I'm sure he'll feel sorry he said all those harsh things."

Spider stared through the doorway at the night sky. Then he looked back at Father. "There's too much to be done. People are angry at the Manchus for the way they handled this war. They'll be a rising soon."

Father took the cup of tea that I had given him and stared at it as if he could see the banners already rising. "Yes, they will. And I won't be there."

Spider sipped some of his tea. "You might not be there in body, but you'll be there in spirit."

"Then do it for both of us." Father bravely raised his cup in a toast. "We'll have our righteous kingdom yet."

"Banish the darkness," Spider said and tossed back his cup of tea.

Father tightened his hand around his cup. "She used to say that so often. So many dreams. So many hopes. Overthrowing the Manchus seemed so easy when we were first married."

"She wouldn't have wanted you to give up," I said urgently.

Father raised his shoulders as if taking new strength from my words. "No, she wouldn't have." He held his cup up to Cousin Spider. "Restore the light." And he finished his.

Chapter Seven

Seven years healed neither the wounds in Father's leg or those in our country. The world didn't come to an end, but it began to crumble bit by bit. The demons asked for more and more, and the Manchus—because they were either cowardly or greedy— gave it to them. Worse yet, the demons' opium began to seep through the countryside like poison through the body of a sick giant. Their filthy drugs began to be sold all across the land—even in our own district.

As Cousin Spider had predicted, the Brotherhood rose up a year later in an area to the northeast. And for a few months we got reports of farmers rallying to their banners; it ate at Father, because the news was always a month old by the time it got to our village.

Sometimes it seemed his soul was prowling restlessly about inside his crippled body like a tiger in a cage, and I didn't know how to stop it. It was even worse when we heard that the uprising had failed and the brothers were being hunted down mercilessly. Father mourned guiltily within our house— as if it were his fault the uprising had failed. He thought it was only a matter of time before the Manchus—or even the demons—came storming into our valley to kill us all.

During those seven years, Father tried to prepare the clan for that terrible day. He gave lessons to anyone who wanted to learn the art of self-defense. He set about reorganizing the militia and drilling them until they were more than just an armed mob.

In the mornings he would try to teach Foxfire and me how to fight. He couldn't wait until we were old enough to take his place in the Brotherhood. He tried to teach us the complicated fighting exercises that he taught to adults. Neither Foxfire nor I was very successful in copying the moves. But even though Foxfire was a year younger than I, he was a boy; and so Father changed. He expected more of Foxfire than of me now. His time for dreams was over.

Foxfire would try and try, but no matter what he did, he could never give Father the perfection he demanded. After seven years both Foxfire and Father had become convinced that Foxfire was clumsy and awkward. Even so, Father wouldn't excuse my little brother from the exercises—Father seemed to be taking out all his disappointments on Foxfire.

I think it bothered Father that Spider hardly ever came by with news of the Brotherhood. Over the years, it was almost as if the Gallant had been forgotten after sacrificing both himself and Mother for the Work. That knowledge ate at his heart like a beetle gnawing at a gourd.

Then the drought came, and we had enough to do just to save ourselves, let alone the country. We counted on heavy rains in the springtime to bring up the first rice crop, but the rain clouds visited us only sparsely. The few clouds that did arrive only sprinkled us with light rains.

I don't think I would have gone down into the fog if times had been normal. But I was worried about our crops and I hoped I could somehow make up to them in attention what they lacked in water.

The fog hung so thick over the courtyard that Father decided we should do our morning exercises inside our house. Though he could no longer perform them with his old speed and grace, he still insisted on trying to do them as best he could. But his lame leg made him slow and clumsy. Of course, he always had Foxfire and me to supervise.

When we had run through them once, I started toward the stove to fill bowls with cold rice. "I'll get breakfast."

"I'm hungry enough to eat the table." Foxfire was going to follow me, but Father caught him by the shoulder and spun him around.

He gave Foxfire the disapproving glare that had become his habit when he looked at my brother now. "No you don't, young man. You looked like a lame buffalo this morning."

Being a year older than Foxfire, I had more co-ordination, and Foxfire suffered from the comparison. But Father had never been that strict with Foxfire before he had gotten his wound. Even if I couldn't restore his leg, I sometimes wished that I could have restored his patience. It probably hadn't helped things that Foxfire had suddenly shot upward in height the last year. He was big for his age, and his gawky frame made it even harder for him. Besides, I think I had more incentive, too. Whenever I felt myself growing tired, I would think of Uncle Windy; and that would give me new energy, because I intended never to depend on anyone's mercy again.

"I did my best," Foxfire said.

Father dragged him back to the center of the room. "And your best wasn't good enough. Half the time it seems like your mind is off walking in the clouds."

Foxfire gave a forlorn shrug. "I can't get my breath control right."

Father gave an exasperated sigh. "Who's the teacher here? You or I?"

"You are, Father, but I was just thinking that maybe it's my technique that's wrong." Foxfire had this dreamy, faraway look on his face, as he did whenever he was getting ready to gab with someone over one of his odd notions. He could spend the entire day discussing the best hardwood to use for a chair or the most effective charm to keep bugs from the plants rather than actually working in the fields.

The words would come tumbling from his lips and his arms would whip around in wild gestures while his mind would flit from one idea to the next like a butterfly flying from one bright flower to another. But it was as if the real Foxfire had already escaped into some secret fortress within his own heart. Father used to laugh at this in the old days, but now he just clapped a hand over Foxfire's mouth before he could babble on. "You let me worry about the theory and technique of the martial arts," Father said. "You just do the exercises the way I taught you."

As I ate a quick breakfast, I watched Foxfire run through the exercises a second time. His arms and legs flailed at the air mechanically until Father threw his hands up in disgust. "That was even worse than the last time. He snatched up a bowl of rice from where I had left it and then picked up a pair of chopsticks. "Do it again." So poor Foxfire had to try it over again while Father ate his breakfast.

But Foxfire was so hungry, the third try proved to be the worst of all. Father shut his eyes as if in pain. "Let's stop before you become hopeless."

Foxfire gratefully took the rice bowl and chopsticks when I handed them to him. "That fog is awfully thick, Cassia. We ought to stay up here."

"It'll burn off soon enough. We may not be able to give our fields much water, but we can at least give them attention. Mother said it was *our* land, after all." I began to rub one of Mother's remedies on a canker sore at one corner of my mouth. Because none of us was eating well, even little things like canker sores did not seem to heal.

He stared at me over his rice bowl. "What're you doing?"

"Mother used to mix herbs with soot and put them on sores." I wiped my hand on a rag.

Father brought his empty rice bowl over to the stove. "Maybe you two shouldn't go outside. I remember a time when Harmony went out in a fog like this and worked the whole morning in a field. When the sun finally came out, he found that he'd been in the wrong field."

"I'll know our fields." I stacked the empty rice bowls together so I could wash them later.

Father sat down stiffly on a bench. "I'm sure that's what Harmony said."

Even in dry weather, his old war wound would sometimes ache painfully, and this damp weather made his leg hurt even more than usual. Damp weather always did that, so I got out a jar of rheumatism ointment I had made up according to Mother's recipe. "It'll be cooler, so we ought to get more done."

"It just looks so miserable out." Foxfire picked up one of his shirts from his usual pile of dirty clothing and began to pull it on. "But if your mind is set to go—"

"It is," I said firmly.

His voice came muffled through the shirt. "Then it's no use arguing."

Father began to roll up his pants leg so he could apply the ointment. "Maybe you'd both better wear extra shirts."

Foxfire's head popped through the opening of the shirt. "Cassia doesn't feel anything through that thick hide of hers."

Ever since that day when Aunt Piety had tried to bind my feet, the clan had teased me mercilessly; so I expected such things from them, but not from my little brother. I tried to defend myself as I got a spare shirt from the wardrobe. "Maybe I don't have any choice. You know Mother left me in charge of you both."

Foxfire finished shoving his hands through the sleeves while he looked at me thoughtfully. He looked sorry he had said anything.

We went out into the courtyard and lifted the sprouting tub, which contained the rice seeds we were trying to sprout for our second rice crop.

Packed with wet straw and rice seed, it was pretty heavy, so we could move only slowly.

The sentry at the village gates stared at us. "You have to be crazy to go out in fog this heavy."

"It's probably only thick up here. It'll thin out once we're down on the valley floor." I jerked at the sprouting tub Foxfire and I were holding between us, and we started down the path that angled back and forth down to the fields.

The path zigzagged so the luck wouldn't flow out of the village, but there were times when I wished it could have been straighter; and this was one of those times as we inched along. I kept waiting for the fog to grow thinner, but it only got thicker as we neared the valley floor.

Even so, I insisted on walking along the tops of the dikes that formed the boundaries as well as paths between the fields. I never thought I could get lost in the rice fields; but then I'd never tried to walk in a fog as thick and as low as this one. It was impossible to see anything but the dirt on top of the dike along which we shuffled.

Finally, I had to give up. "Let's put the tub down."

Though he was on the other side of the sprouting tub, Foxfire was a blurred shape—like some puppet from a shadow play I had once seen. "I was wondering when we were going to rest. It's heavy having to carry this tub and our hoes too." Setting his end of the tub down with a thump, he sidled around it so he could see me.

I looked around for landmarks, but I couldn't see any. "I think we're wandering. Doesn't the river sound way too close?"

I couldn't make out his features until he was standing so close to me that our hips were touching. He complained, "There has to be a better way of life than this, where we have to fight for every scrap of land and every bit of fertilizer and every grain of rice."

Knowing what was coming, I heaved a big sigh. "Now don't start on one of your money-making schemes again."

"But this one will work for sure." He licked his lips. "What if we saved the seed from the best plants? Eventually we'd have better crops and could command better prices."

I didn't let myself get mad at my little brother. He'd already gotten enough scolding from Father this morning. Besides, his face had the same excited, dreamy expression Mother's face had had when she began one of her tales. For her sake, I tried to act like a good big sister. "If we kept out our best seed,"

I explained, "we wouldn't get much money for the seed that we did sell. And we'd starve long before we could grow those super plants of yours."

But he went on. "Well, maybe we could save just a handful of seed, then."

"With the drought on, we'll need every bit of seed we grow." He looked so downcast that I patted his arm affectionately. "But it's a thought whenever we do have a little cash to spare."

"It always comes down to money," he grumbled.

Suddenly a woman screamed in the distance. "It's Phoenixes," she began shouting. "The Phoenixes are attacking."

The Phoenixes were the large, rich clan from the next valley who had been feuding with our clan, the Youngs, for hundreds of years. My brother looked all around us as if he expected a Phoenix to pop out of the fog at any moment. "What do we do? Hide until the militia finds us?"

"That could take forever in this fog. I think we ought to try to get back to the village." I shifted my grip on the shaft of my hoe so it could be used as weapon—just as Father had taught us. "And we kill any Phoenix that gets in our way."

"Oh." Foxfire lifted his own hoe from his shoulder uncertainly.

"Don't hold your hoe that way. Or when you swing, you'll take off your head. It isn't the handsomest one around, but I'm rather fond of it right where it is—on top of your neck." I reached out a hand and rotated the shaft of his hoe so that he would no longer cut himself.

Both of us jumped when the woman let out a pure, high animal wail. "Some righteous kingdom this is." His knuckles tightened around the shaft so that they showed an almost bone white.

The woman stopped abruptly, and I didn't like the idea of what that might mean. Then the sentry at our village gates began to beat the alarm gong. "There. That should give us a general bearing. We're bound to reach the east side of the valley." Our village of Three Willows lay halfway up the slope.

"But what about the tub?" Foxfire asked.

"We'll just have to leave it." I started to trot along the dikes. I started to worry about what we were going to do if we met Phoenixes. I was fairly sure I could defend myself; but Foxfire was another matter. "You'd better let me do the fighting if we meet any Phoenixes."

"Sometimes you and Father make me feel like so much useless baggage," he complained.

I hated to make my little brother lose any more

confidence in himself, so I glanced over my shoulder. "You're not as bad as you and Father seem to think. But you need more practice." Suddenly, the dike took an unexpected twist to my right, so my feet were hovering in the empty air instead of on hard-packed dirt. With a cry, I landed on top of the eggplants someone had growing between the dike and the first ridge of rice plants. Foxfire came crashing down a moment later beside me.

I sat up, spitting the dirt from my mouth, just as a shadowy figure loomed over us. I sprang to my feet, the hoe feeling twice as heavy as normal as I raised it over my shoulder menacingly.

And then I noticed that the person was wearing ordinary cloth shoes with little red lightning bolts embroidered into the tops. I recognized them because I had done the embroidery myself.

"Father?" I whispered incredulously. Crippled leg and all, he had come looking for us.

Father jammed his spear blade first into the dirt. "Thank Heaven you're alive," he said softly, and squatted down so I could see his relieved smile.

I took his hand when he extended it and let myself be pulled up beside him. When he started to give me a quick hug, I held him back. "Wait. I'll get soot all over you."

"It doesn't matter," he said, and crushed my face against his familiar, threadbare coat.

"It's a wonder that you ever found us in this fog. Mother's spirit must have guided you." Foxfire climbed up on the dike and gratefully spread one arm out to hug Father too.

Father gave a good-natured tweak to Foxfire's ear and then pushed us both away. "It was easy to find you two. You were blundering along like a pair of drunken pigs." He began to rub his bad leg. I was sure that the mist in the valley wasn't doing it any good. "It's a good thing I didn't wait for the militia to muster."

"But why didn't the morning patrol warn us?" I asked.

"I found the patrol leader back in his home. He said it was so foggy, they didn't think the Phoenixes would be out." Father grimaced. As head of the militia, it was his responsibility to defend the valley.

I was trying to find something that would comfort him when a shadow suddenly appeared in the misty fields to our right. "Father," I shouted, "behind you."

Yanking his spear from the dirt, Father tried to whirl around like a tiger; but his bad leg dragged in the dirt, slowing his movements. Still, he managed to parry the sword stroke with the blade of his spear.

He and the intruder clashed together with a metallic ring that echoed through the valley.

Foxfire stood there with his mouth open. I caught hold of his collar and jerked him back. "Give Father some room."

Father might be crippled in one leg, but he had lost none of his old fighting skills. I watched as he twisted his shoulders slightly, backhanding the spear shaft up and above his shoulder so that the butt of his spear came thudding down against the swordsman's skull. The man fell backward, disappearing into the fog. He landed with a loud, crunching noise among the invisible rice plants.

But before we could even begin to crow about Father's triumph, more shadows materialized like ghosts—both on our right and on our left.

Chapter Eight

Our voices—though low—had drawn a patrol of Phoenixes.

"We're surrounded." With the best and bravest of intentions, Foxfire started to swing his hoe up to his shoulder for a blow against the Phoenixes.

I barely ducked in time. Grabbing the seat of his trousers, I shook it. "You'd better leave the fighting to Father and me. You can't talk your way through a battle."

Foxfire could pick the worst times to play the proud, stubborn fool. "But you just said I wasn't as bad at fighting as I thought."

"And you're not." I tried to find some way to

salvage his pride. "You just need more practice, that's all."

Foxfire lowered his hoe dejectedly. "I'm not bad."

Father adjusted his grip on his spear. "You may have the heart of a warrior, but you don't have the hands and feet. Let your sister and me handle this."

"I'm all set." I straightened, raising my hoe over my shoulder.

"The baggage train is ready too," Foxfire mumbled.

"Then here we go." Father began to limp forward while we followed, moving in tiny steps so that we wouldn't bump into him.

Suddenly we burst into one of those freak pockets within the fog where the mist thinned. A Phoenix stepped deliberately on top of the dike. Father's spear shaft clacked against his while Foxfire squatted down, trying to keep out of Father's way. And then I was too busy to watch my brother as a young Phoenix suddenly came high-stepping out of a field.

I can remember seeing his angry face, mouth contorted in a shout, his queue done up in a knot at the back of his head. There was a birthmark on his cheek in the shape of a berry, and it seemed to burn a bright purple. It was the first time I had ever seen one of our ancient enemies, and I remember feeling startled because he didn't have monstrous horns or scales. In fact, he looked like any boy in our own clan.

I had time to parry the blow from his sword, though its force made my arms feel numb. Then I managed a counterstroke, chopping at his leg with the blade of my hoe. Startled, the boy jumped back so that he fell among the rice plants.

In front of me, I heard Father give a familiar grunt—a little technique he used to concentrate the energy in his body. There was a loud clang, and the Phoenix gave a cry as his own spear went flying from his hands. He jumped from the dike, crashing noisily through the rice plants as he ran.

Father began to shuffle forward again, twisting his head this way and that, ready for another attack. "Come on." I nudged Foxfire with my hoe. He rose and started after Father.

I looked around but saw no Phoenixes. "We've scared them off," I crowed.

"No." Father didn't slow down at all. "They probably have their orders. They're to drive off those they can't kill easily. Then they can work whatever mischief they have planned for our fields."

Ten meters on, we could not even see them, though I was sure they were prowling about somewhere in the mist, ready to intercept us if we tried to go back.

"Where's our militia?" Foxfire asked the same question that had been bothering me. "Those slow-pokes should have been down here by now."

Father sounded worried. "I don't know what's keeping them, but we'd better see what we can do to hurry them along."

Though his old war wound must have pained him terribly, Father stumped along the dike tops as fast as he could until the three of us were panting raggedly. He wouldn't even stop to catch his breath when we finally reached the terraced fields that marked the eastern slope of the valley. It was as if his soul were raging at a weak body that could only limp when he wanted to race.

I wished our mother were still alive. I felt sure that she would have been able to soothe some of Father's anger; but I didn't know what to do. I could only watch as Father pushed himself along.

A quarter of the way up the slope, the terraced fields gave way to peach trees where stray wisps of mist hung from the branches like torn shrouds. It was only after Father had stumbled several times over the roots that he finally began to use his spear to support himself in the struggle up the steep incline. "Why haven't we met patrols? I told them to send some squads out."

I tried to keep pace by his elbow, ready to catch him. "Maybe the Phoenixes are up here too."

I almost gave a shout of relief when we finally cleared the trees. Beyond the ditch were the old, worn bricks of the wall that surrounded our village. The wall itself was one of the oldest things in the village. It had been built generations ago, and each generation had added to it until it now stood some three meters high with a dirt rampart inside and a watchtower by the village gates.

"We must be at the south wall," Father murmured, and began to hobble along toward the south wall, where the gates faced the valley. He looked down in disgust as we skirted the ditch. "Look at this." Father gestured toward the sides of the ditch, which had crumbled into easy slopes. "We're going to have to make the sides steeper." He pointed all around. "I've been after them for years to put stakes in the bottoms of the ditches." He clicked his tongue in exasperation as his eyes swept the walls. "And there's no one watching for a sneak attack."

In the distance we could hear the shrill voice of the Golden Cat scolding the militia. "What are you waiting for? Hand-written invitations? Go on and fight the Phoenixes. He's just one man. He can't stop all of you."

"How could one man frighten the whole militia?" I asked Father.

"One man could—if it was the right man," Father explained. "It's one thing for them to face bandits or other farmers. It's another thing for them to face a professional warrior."

When we rounded the corner, we saw it really was only one man who was defying the clan. He didn't look like he came from around here, though. He was tall and pale, and his shoulders hunched as if he were huddling by some invisible fire that could drive away the terrible, freezing cold that surrounded him. There was a short sword hanging from a baldric down his back with the hilt just behind the right shoulder. And his black trousers were tucked into a pair of white stockings.

"I'm warning you: Don't set one foot outside of these gates until my hosts are finished down below. Be good neighbors and let them borrow a little rice." He spoke in an odd, monotonous accent of the ancient northern provinces. In a way, it reminded me of the way Aster spoke.

"Dusty," Father murmured sadly.

"Who?" I asked.

But at that moment a middle-aged man slipped out of the crowd. Next to Father, I think Uncle Blacky was the most conscientious member of the militia. Only his father's death had kept him from taking the government exams. As it was, he still tried to keep up his studies after working in his family's fields. Somehow he even found time to take self-defense lessons from Father as well.

Nervously he spread his feet and then looked down to make sure he was in the right stance. The hands that held his rake were smudged from the ink he made himself. "I'll fight you if no one else will."

Dusty merely wriggled his fingers for Uncle Blacky to advance. "Come on then. I haven't got all day."

Suddenly a ten-year-old boy shoved his way through the crowd. "The Youngs. The Youngs." Waving a stick over his head, he charged past Uncle Blacky.

"Come back here, Cricket." In alarm, Uncle Blacky chased after his son.

It was as if Dusty had been saving all his energy for this one encounter. Without even bothering to draw his sword, he stiffened his spine, elbows and knees bending easily, metamorphosing from a man into a mantis. Before Uncle Blacky could even plant his feet for a swing of the rake, Dusty punched him.

"The Ginger Hand," he called out merrily—as if he were announcing the name of a dance step rather than a blow. Then he knocked Cricket backward with a slap. "The Lion Playing." Still flowing in the same motion, Dusty settled his arms and legs into the next position while father and son lay groaning at his feet.

"What about you now?" He nodded to the Golden Cat, who was standing safely on the wall. "Can you fight as well as you talk?" When the Golden Cat remained where he was, Dusty spat contemptuously in the dirt. "I didn't think so." He lowered his eyes to the militia again. "Isn't there anyone in this pigsty who's willing to fight?"

"I guess it's up to me." Father limped forward with quiet dignity. He didn't have a general's costume or banners or a band to play for him; but he could not have marched any straighter or taller than he did at that moment. "The mantis eats the little beetles, not knowing that the crane is watching," Father quoted the old proverb. He himself belonged to the White Crane school of fighting.

Dusty dropped his hands as if he were surprised to see Father. "What are you doing here?"

"This is my clan's village." Father stopped about two meters away.

"I'm visiting some friends who want to improve their martial skills and needed some instruction." Embarrassed, Dusty gestured in the direction of the Phoenix village.

Father spread out his legs, bending his knees slightly. "I wish you had visited me first."

"I didn't know you were here." Dusty scratched the back of his neck uncomfortably, as if he didn't enjoy this reunion at all. "Now it's too late. I promised to help my hosts."

Father wound his queue around his neck so that it wouldn't get in his way if he had to fight. He hadn't had any time to do that before when we were battling the Phoenixes below. "Hosts? Let's drop the fancy name, shall we? You were hired to do their dirty work for them."

Dusty stiffened ever so slightly. "Money's scarce and so is food." He added softly, "And 'hosts' are even scarcer."

Father shook his head. "We once swore an oath of brotherhood. We carried on the Work together. So how can you help my enemies against me?"

"I gave my word to them." With great dignity, he drew his sword.

"So you serve whoever feeds your belly, is that it?" Father snapped his spear up into the first attack position.

"We were friends once." Dusty held out a hand toward Father as if begging him not to go any further. "Don't make me humiliate you now."

"I'm here to defend my home." Father tried to put the weight on his good leg as he lunged. But Dusty was simply too quick for him, stepping to the side as he grabbed the shaft of Father's spear. A quick jerk and Father was pulled off-balance. He went sprawling forward into the dirt.

Dusty cleared his throat. "I don't enjoy making a spectacle out of you. But I keep my word once I agree to help someone."

It was obvious that all of Father's cunning and skills didn't count against another old veteran like Dusty; but still Father wouldn't give up. "Let's try that again, shall we?" In a grim display of determination, Father used his spear to help him get to his feet.

With a lithe motion, Dusty almost squatted down, his buttocks resting on his left heel while he swept his right leg around to trip Father. This time Father fell on his back.

Dusty leaped forward, bringing his heel down

over Father's throat, ready to crush it; but he paused, drawing his eyebrows together as if he were both puzzled and a bit frightened at Father's persistence. "You might have been a good fighter once, but can't you see?" He squinted sadly at Father. "You're not anymore. The demons saw to that."

Father caught sight of Foxfire and me from the corner of his eye. For our sake, perhaps, he felt that he had to make another effort. "I can keep this up longer than you can." He tried to bring his spear up.

But Dusty stepped back and his right foot darted out, kicking the spear from Father's grasp. It rattled against the ground several meters away. Father rolled onto his stomach, ready to crawl after it.

Dusty glided in between Father and the spear. "Face it. The demons destroyed you."

"Not my heart and not my spirit." Father struggled to his hands and knees.

Dusty shook his head slowly. "Don't make me kill you." He swung round then to point toward the gaping militia. "Remember: I'll be down there with my hosts, so don't you dare leave this village." Then, twisting around, he strolled leisurely down the path into the mist as if Father didn't even exist.

And that probably hurt Father's pride the worst of all.

Chapter Nine

Father was on his hands and knees by the time I got to him. But when I reached out a hand to help him up, he shook me off. "I'm sorry that you had to see me made into a clown." And, shoving himself up, he tried to rise as if he were still the tall, proud, nimble man who had marched off to war against the demons. But his leg gave out again as he slipped and fell.

Instinctively, I put out my hand once again to support him. "The footing's terrible here."

Red-faced, Father took my hand. "The demons certainly haven't helped my leg any."

Father was just straightening up when we heard

the first faint hissing sound from the valley. It was followed by a swish and then a short series of rattles. The noise swelled gradually in volume until it sounded as if the fields were filled with snakes.

My stomach tightened as I recognized the sounds. "The Phoenixes are stealing our crops," I murmured.

The hiss came from the hard, crisp slicing of hand scythes through bunches of rice stalks and the swish as the plants were knocked against the mouths of the threshing boxes. The rice grains rattled as they dropped through the screen to the bottom.

I shook my head, hardly daring to believe our enemies would go this far. But then they had always been arrogant. Their valley, which was so much wider and greener than ours, gave them larger harvests. As a result, they had the tea money—as bribes were called—to make the officials look the other way when the Phoenixes bullied and terrorized the district.

"Are you going to let them get away with that?" Father's eyes surveyed the people by the gates and along the village wall.

I stared down at the forbidding gray blanket beneath me. The entire village of Phoenixes could have been hiding there, so I didn't exactly enjoy the thought of going down to our fields. And I wasn't the only one.

Uncle Blacky and Cricket got to their feet; refusing to look at Father, they limped back into the village. It was clear that they didn't think they could defeat Dusty, nor did the rest of the clan. They refused to budge.

When no one joined Father, he flung a desperate hand toward the mist. "This fog can work to our advantage: We form small squads to hit their harvesters hard and then run back into the mists. It won't take long before the Phoenixes get discouraged and leave."

Stony, the Golden Cat's spoiled son, shoved his way to the front of the crowd at the gate. Though he was only a militia man, he was dressed up as finely as any general in red felt boots, padded vest and helmet. There was an expensive cutlass in his hand. He'd tried a number of times to use his father's influence so he could replace Father. But though Stony liked to dress like a warrior, he didn't have the heart of one. "And what would happen if we met your old friend?" he asked Father. "I doubt if he'd be so kind the next time."

I asked myself then what my mother would have done; I knew the answer almost at once: She wouldn't have hesitated to go with Father—no matter what the consequences might be. She'd always said that honor was more important than life.

I gave the clan a withering, contemptuous look. "He can't fight us all."

Father lifted his head a little, as if gathering new confidence. "My daughter's a better warrior than any of you."

"Don't use that venomous little creature to shame us. It's that wild serpent blood of her mother's that's just coming out again." Stony jerked his head at me. "She's a serpent's child if there ever was one." More than a few heads nodded their agreement.

My hand tightened around my hoe. Ever since that day when I wouldn't let Uncle Windy bind my feet, the clan had treated my brother and me like two wild creatures; and they often tried to use my mother's serpent ancestry to insult me.

As usual, though, I tried to turn my bloodline to my advantage. "Serpents may crawl on their bellies, but they aren't cowards. They always get their revenge even if they have to die. We'll show you what honor means at least to one family. We'll drive them out single-handed if we have to. Do you think the warriors in our family end with Father?"

There was a strange tingling sensation in the air—

the same charged feeling after a lightning bolt smashes against the ground. About a dozen militiamen shuffled their feet and looked at one another as if they were ashamed of themselves.

And my heart began to race. Perhaps the sight of the two of us marching together might shame the others into following us. And maybe we'd even have enough fighters to harass the Phoenixes into leaving. Surely it would be a deed worthy of being recorded in the clan book.

Foxfire stepped forward, looking frightened and yet determined at the same time. I thought it was going to be just like the time when we were children and had defied the entire clan. I was surprised when he shook his head instead. "Cassia, this isn't some cheap street singer's ballad. There's no sense dying for your pride."

Only Heaven knows how he had gathered up enough nerve to speak up in public; but it couldn't have come at a worse time. I jabbbed my hoe at him. "If you won't help us, at least keep quiet."

Foxfire looked beyond me to Father. "If you won't think of yourself, Father, then think of Cassia. You know what could happen if the Phoenixes caught her."

"I can take care of myself," I declared hotly. "They

won't take me alive if it comes to that." But I could feel the old familiar resentment welling up inside me whenever the subject of my sex was brought up. It's one thing for a woman to do all sorts of heroics in a story; it's quite another for a girl to practice the martial arts with the boys—and beat them.

For once, though, Stony eagerly agreed with my brother. He was just glad of an excuse to keep from going down into the valley. "Do you really want to condemn your daughter to . . . to that?"

I scowled at them. "Better than living the rest of my days with my head hanging down in shame."

Suddenly I felt Father's hand on my shoulder. "Such a big heart in such a small body." I turned to see the warm sadness in his eyes. "Hearts like yours must be saved and cherished."

"I'm going down with you," I insisted stubbornly.

"I could order you to stay." He squeezed my shoulder.

I stared up at him. "It's the one order from you that I would disobey. Tie me up and lock me in a room, and I'll still find a way of coming down after you."

He pursed his lips thoughtfully for a moment and then looked beyond me toward the clan, as if he were weighing my value against that of our kin. He gave a heavy sigh. "Maybe we ought to save ourselves for the more important fights ahead." He smiled bitterly. "If something happened to us, who would continue the Work in Three Willows?"

I realized that Father was trying to find a way to save both our honors. "Someone has to be a witness to the truth," I agreed.

"Yes, that's right." He let go of my shoulder. It was hard to put the tiger back into the cage like that, but he managed to gain control of himself. "Well"— he rubbed a finger up and down his throat self-consciously—"I think I'll go home and brew some tea."

I could certainly understand why Father might want to escape from this shameful scene. "I'll make it for you."

"No." Father's voice caught so that it was more of a rasp. "I'd rather be alone for a while, if you don't mind."

My eyes searched his face. I think it was harder fighting his own pride than battling Dusty. "If that's what you'd rather do."

"Yes. You be my eyes and ears for what happens next." Father picked up his spear.

Foxfire swallowed. "Father, I'm sorry."

Father wagged his finger from side to side. "Never apologize if you think you did the right thing."

"Yes, sir." Foxfire nodded his head miserably.

"Just don't expect me to thank you." Showing almost as much courage as when he marched out to meet Dusty, Father now turned his back on the Phoenixes and limped toward the gates—no longer the proud warrior but only a tired, crippled veteran.

Quickly, as if afraid of being contaminated by his madness, the militia parted for him, making way on either side so that he could pass through a narrow lane.

I waited until Father was out of sight before I went after Foxfire. "Fool. Traitor. Coward."

Lifting his arms protectively over his head, Foxfire danced back out of range of my hoe. "Do you think I enjoyed adding to Father's humiliation? I was just trying to save you," he complained. "There was a time when you didn't mind me doing that. We could only count on one another then."

I paused in mid stride and forced myself to take a deep breath as I remembered the promises I had made so long ago. "It was us against the whole clan then."

His arms still guarding his face, Foxfire nodded

his head as if he were eager to make up with me. "It still is, Cassia." He parted his arms so that he could peek out at me.

I thought of what Stony had said about us, and then I studied Foxfire's face with its high, flat forehead and the narrow eyes and the long, slender nose. It was Mother's face and it was my face too. And I reminded myself of that promise I had made long ago that we would never be separated—no matter what. It wasn't the first time that I'd had to recall that moment, but this may have been the most difficult.

Still, whether I liked it or not, Mother had said we were both of the same blood and fortune. "I guess so," I sighed sadly.

Chapter Ten

It was late in the morning before the summer sun began to burn off the mist. By that time the Phoenixes had left our valley. The militia found the corpse of the woman who had been screaming in the mist. She'd been killed not far from where the river ran down the sloping rocks into our valley. Some of the militia, at least, had enough courage to carry her back up to the village.

Our search for our sprouting tub took us into the prime fields where the Phoenixes had concentrated their efforts. Some of the owners or their tenants scurried about, staring in disbelief. Where there had once been fine, tall plants there was now only rice straw strewn all about. The villagers looked as if they were in some nightmare from which they would wake at any moment.

When I finally caught sight of our tub, it was lying on its side. "Oh, no." And I started to race along the dike tops.

"Why didn't they just take our seed?" Foxfire had stayed right behind me.

"Maybe they saw what poor quality it was." But it wasn't nearly as bad as I had first thought, because someone had made an effort to scoop the seed and the rice straw together into a pile.

"Well, at least one of the Phoenixes has a conscience." Foxfire squatted down and began to separate the little rice seeds with their tiny green sprouts from the pieces of straw.

We righted the tub and began to repack it, putting down a layer of rice straw first and then a layer of rice seeds and following that with more straw and so on. Next to us, Uncle Windy and Stony had been carrying on a quiet discussion. Suddenly Uncle Windy's voice rose almost to a shriek. "How can you expect me to pay you the full rent?" He collapsed to his knees and flung a handful of straw and dirt into the air. "The Phoenixes have taken everything. Everything."

"Uncle Windy's in trouble," I whispered. I took no pleasure in his predicament, because it was one we might be in.

Stony hovered over him unhappily. "But my father has to pay the taxes on our fields." He slapped his hands helplessly against his sides. "What are we supposed to do? Tell the magistrate to collect from the Phoenixes?"

I finished packing the straw over the top of the tub. "Well, they always say that the Golden Cat lands on his feet no matter what happens."

"But he's *our* landlord too." Foxfire grasped one of the handles of the tub. "What are we going to do if our crops are stolen too?"

"First of all, let's see if the Phoenixes even bothered with them." With my hoe in my left hand, I took the handle in my right and nodded to Foxfire to help me carry the tub.

Instinctively, we both headed for the field where Mother had died. On our way, we stopped by a small pond near the east slope. Normally at this time of year it was filled with rainwater, but this year it was barely half full.

Like his older brother, Spider, Sticks took after his bony mother, so it was hard to believe that he could work the water pump all by himself. He was feeding water from the pond to one of their terraced fields of vegetables. The pump was a low, narrow trough through which a "chain" of wooden boards ran, sweeping the water along as he worked the pedals. It was hard, backbreaking work that would leave his feet sore and blistered by the time he was finished; but it was better than having to water plants by hand the way we had to.

He leaned against the support bar in an elaborate show of weariness. "I wish I'd gone over the wall and joined One-Eye." One-Eye was the vicious beast who led a band of bandits that terrorized the district.

We set the tub down, and I started to fill it with water from a gourd that was tied to the tub's right handle. The water would gradually trickle through the layers of seed and straw and then out through a hole at the bottom of the tub. We would take the tub home at the end of the day when the water had drained out. "Why not join your brother and carry on the Work?" I asked.

"There's more future in being a bandit."

"And what makes you think that you'd enjoy life with One-Eye?" I doubted if One-Eye would have tolerated all his chatter.

"Anything would be better than this." Sweat was dotting his face as his feet moved from pedal to pedal. He looked as if he were running in slow motion, but, of course, he never moved.

"That's for sure," Foxfire agreed.

If I had let him, Foxfire would have gone on exchanging complaints for the rest of the day with Sticks. "Why don't you go inspect our fields?" I suggested. "I'll catch up with you in a moment."

If Foxfire hadn't been worried about the fields himself, I think he might have argued with me. As it was, he started off again at a trot.

When he was gone, Sticks laughed at us. "You've got to stop being his nursemaid, Cassia."

I sipped the last of the water in the gourd. "He's too clever for his own good. The least little thing distracts him."

The pump creaked steadily as Sticks continued to step on the pedals. "That may be. But sometime you're going to have to get married and leave him on his own."

"No one will want a bossy wife." Wiping my mouth on my sleeve, I picked up my hoe and got up. "So no one will want me."

"There must be some deaf old man who's desperate enough," Sticks called after me, but I kept on walking.

Foxfire was just standing there when I reached

him. I sank to my knees when I saw what the Phoenixes had done. "I hope they get sick as dogs on what they stole."

I had been growing squash and beans on our side of the dikes. Once the dirt had been covered with vines and leaves, but now there were only long, ragged holes where the Phoenixes had ripped them out. Worse yet, though our rice hadn't been good enough to steal, nearly half of our plants had been trampled down into the dirt. "It looks like the whole clan marched through here," I complained. "It would have been bad enough if they had *stolen* our rice, but just to waste it like this." I felt angry enough to march over the ridge and attack the first Phoenix I saw.

Foxfire jumped down into the field with a determined look on his face. "We'd better prop up what we can so it doesn't spoil."

Aster, who still rented a field on our right, tried to cheer me up the way she always did. "Why do the Phoenixes have to have such big feet anyway?"

Compared to her troubles, I knew I didn't have any right to be angry over the loss of my vegetables. Cholera and other illnesses had killed off most of her family, and scurvy had carried off her last relative except for her husband, Tiny. And yet Aster never lost her cheerful way of looking at things. Despite all that, I couldn't help complaining to her. "But don't you want to get even with the Phoenixes?"

"Of course, but I'm being practical about it. I just pretend that every nasty little weed I yank out is the head of a Phoenix." She waved a handful of green plants at me.

"Anger is a luxury for the poor," Tiny added. He was tall, with shoulders and arms well muscled from smithing, and his hoe looked almost like a toy in those big hands of his. Though he was a man of twenty, he was good friends with Foxfire, and the two of them talked about any subject under the sun.

I stripped off the extra shirt I had put on this morning. "What are you doing down here, Tiny?"

"I don't think he trusts me to grow food for him anymore." Aster raised her head so I could see her face underneath the wide, crownless straw hat with the little cloth valance all around its edge. "Tiny says he's going to grow the rice himself."

Tiny was a calm, peaceful man, the way some big men can be. "You can't make the plants grow just by gossiping to them," he explained to his wife and then glanced at me. "Besides, no one has any orders for me. Or the means to pay."

Aster let the corners of her mouth droop comically

at that moment. "I think you're just making that up so you can get away from the forge." When Tiny merely grunted, Aster rested the shaft of the hoe against her legs and held up her hands, palms turned upward, as if presenting Tiny to us for the first time. "How can I have an intelligent discussion when all he'll do is grunt?"

"He just has a lot of natural dignity," Foxfire defended his friend. He spent every moment of his spare time up at the forge—even when he was supposed to be practicing the drills with me.

"He's got enough for all of us." Aster laughed and then squinted at the soot-covered canker sore on my face. "Cassia, are you wearing some new kind of makeup?"

Foxfire answered before I could. "She's got to do something. I don't think Father and I can count on having some groom pay us to take her away." He ducked the clod of dirt I threw at him. "The only way we're ever going to marry her off is to throw in a big dowry."

"Well"—I made a face at him—"that's not going to happen in a long while."

"Maybe it'll happen sooner than you think." Foxfire stayed crouched down low so that he was a smaller target. "I've been thinking that if the rest of our fields are like this, I ought to go away—like Harmony."

Harmony had been one of those who had left the valley to look for work at the start of the drought. There was a new city the demons were building to the northeast across from the old one that belonged to the Portuguese. He had boasted of the money he was going to send home to his family, but so far the remittances had been few and far between.

I knew I should have been more patient with Foxfire—as Mother would have been. But instead, I got angry and scared all at the same time—angry because he wanted to desert us right when we needed him the most and scared becasue I was afraid of what would happen to my little brother once he was out of my sight. It took me a moment to find my voice. "Of all the crazy schemes you've ever had, this one is the dumbest. How can you even think of leaving the valley? One of our ancestors died in this same field. And so did Mother."

Foxfire stood on his left leg as he started to scratch his right foot. "That doesn't mean we have to starve to death too. Sometimes I feel like Sticks on the water chain: No matter how hard we work, we just stay in one place."

I picked up one rice plant and tried to straighten

it. When I let it go, it drooped; but at least it was off the ground. "Harmony is the last one I'd imitate. He ran off and left his children to the clan's charity."

Foxfire balanced on one leg for a moment like some big, unhappy crane. "I could always try someplace else."

"What places could you go that Harmony already hasn't? Don't you understand? You're better off staying here." I reached down and scooped up a handful of dirt. Foxfire started to duck again, but I simply held the dirt out to him. "This is our home. This is our flesh and blood. Leaving here is like trying to run away from yourself."

Most of the time Foxfire would listen to me with his good-humored, long-suffering look. But there were times when he showed some of the same restless spirit that possessed Father. "How can you say that after what Uncle Windy and Aunt Piety tried to do to you? The rest of the clan thought we were crazy. Remember?"

I shrugged. "I suppose in their own minds they meant well. It's really a question of educating them to what's right."

"How are we going to educate them? The clan just laughs at us, and they'll be laughing even more after this morning." He set his foot down. "Aren't you tired of being treated like the village idiots?"

It was hard to say whether he was ashamed of Father or of himself. But whatever the cause, I wished there were some way to reach into his souls and wipe the shame away—to see that Foxfire was safe and protected from all harm and pain. Mother had always had the knack of saying the right thing to ease someone's hurt. It made me feel helpless and frustrated that all I could do was lamely repeat her words. "The clan will come around once they realize we're telling the truth about things. How are we going to achieve anything if we run away? Remember the White Serpent."

"I know. I know. A child of hers would never give up." He rubbed a hand roughly back and forth beneath his throat, almost as if he were trying to saw himself in two. "It's just that I feel like I'll suffocate if I don't get away from here."

Foxfire's words frightened me almost as much as Dusty had—though I wasn't going to admit that to my brother. Instead, I tamped the dirt down with the flat of my hand. "Farmers should be like their plants," I declared. "They should always stay where their roots are."

Chapter Eleven

After we had done what we could for our first field, we checked the other four and found that they weren't as bad. But since we counted on almost every grain of rice and vegetable to use either as food or for seed or rent, any loss brought us nearer to disaster. No one would be able to have second helpings on rice anymore, and I would have to cut back on the number of vegetables I used for meals. We wouldn't be able to have more than a few bites to help flavor our rice.

Foxfire could tell that I was worried, but I didn't want to tell him why. It would only have started him thinking about running away again. Instead, I took him back to the first field with me to prepare one corner. Later, after we'd harvested the first rice crop, we would transplant the seedlings of the second crop to the ridges.

We had just started to work there when a girl cried out, "What happened to your face, Cassia?"

To my annoyance, I saw it was Peony, clutching a basket in both her hands while she gaped at me. Even if I could have forgiven her for refusing to help me escape the matchmaker, I can't say we would have been the best of friends. Her mind was full of hairdos and clothes and romance stories, so any serious talk from me simply puzzled her.

But despite all that nonsense that filled her mind (or perhaps because of it), she got along well with the other girls—while I could not. Still, I found I couldn't get too angry with her. It would have been like boxing with a butterfly. And Mother had always made a point of getting along with even the silliest of females.

I closed my eyes and murmured to myself a sentence I remembered Mother saying: "We are spiritual sisters with everyone of our sex. We are spiritual sisters. We are spiritual sisters."

Peony leaned forward over the field anxiously. "Are you all right, Cassia?"

Tired of answering questions about the cure, I brushed my sleeve lightly across the sooty spot. "Sometimes the cure is more embarrassing than the disease."

"Oh, I see." She blinked her eyes when she saw the sore. I couldn't help but contrast it to her own clear complexion. And even though we'd had all that trouble this morning, she had taken the time to do her hair up with a red silk ribbon. "How've you been eating, Cassia, Foxfire?" she said to us. But like the rest of the clan, she refused to say anything to the Strangers—she ignored Aster and Tiny. "Are you saving your weeds?"

I glanced at Foxfire, wondering if he still wanted to follow in Harmony's footsteps; but he did his best to ignore me. If Peony was gathering weeds, she was probably going to boil them for what the clan called grass soup—the last resort for a starving family. But then, after today's raid, it would be hard for even the richest families to give food to Peony.

"No, not today." Foxfire tried to smile encouragingly.

"That's good." Peony sighed in relief. "I didn't want to go looking in the hills for weeds—not with the Phoenixes all around."

"You're welcome to take what you can find." I

began to build up the mound that would separate the corner from the rest of the field.

Peony, however, had remained where she was. "Would you mind helping me pick them?" She looked down uncertainly at the dirt in the field. "I'd do it myself, but I have this rash between my toes."

"I still have a lot of ointments that my mother made up. I'm sure I could find one to cure you." I smiled maliciously.

"No, no." She shuffled back hastily. "I don't want you to waste your medicine on me."

The hot, humid air wasn't helping my mood any. "Well, you don't expect us to find the weeds for you, do you?"

"Don't make such a fuss." Foxfire began to move across the ridges. "You and Father are always saying how we have to unite and help one another."

I pointed my finger at him furiously. Peony always played helpless, so someone usually took pity on her. "I wish you'd remember that when I ask you to fetch water."

He looked at me innocently—as if his conscience were perfectly clear on the subject. "I do, don't I?"

"And what about yesterday?" I demanded.

He paused, looking irritated. "I got the water."

"Only after I threatened you with the broom," I

said. But I was beginning to feel big and ugly and clumsy and a nag compared to "sweet, little" Peony. I suppose someone like her would always make me feel that way when she was around. The sooner we gave her what she wanted, the sooner she'd be gone and we could get back to the work at hand.

"All right." I plucked a blade of sword calamus that had just begun to grow and wiped off a bit of dirt from the tiny, red, scorpionlike root. "Here." I held it up like a hunting trophy. "This will be a little biting to the taste, but it's not dangerous." I patted the ridge smooth and firm with my foot.

"Wait. I think I've found a little fat pig hiding in the dirt." Foxfire pretended to reach intently toward the edge of the dike. "Ah, there we are." He began squealing like a pig and his hands shook as if the two stems of ear-scoop grass were wriggling as he uprooted them from their bed of dirt. The upper parts of the stems were shaped like the tiny scoops that barbers use to get the wax out of people's ears. But the tiny blue flowers themselves were still just buds along the stems.

"Thank you." Peony dimpled prettily. She took the grass from him and shook the stems so that the dirt sprinkled the ground.

I handed the sword calamus to Peony and then

pointed at some small, white, barred flowers, called shepherd's purse, that grew by the dike. "You can eat that too. It won't be quite as biting as the sword calamus."

"Oh, good." Peony squatted down, but it was just beyond her reach. Even though she looked perfectly capable of climbing down into the field, Foxfire was about to help her, when suddenly we heard a commotion at the mouth of the valley.

For a moment I thought it was the Phoenixes and I got ready to run; but though we couldn't hear what they were saying, the people didn't sound frightened.

"Now what's wrong?" I frowned.

"I'll be back in a moment." Foxfire threw down his hoe and went dashing off.

"Hey," I called after him.

Though he was twenty, Tiny could still be like a little boy. "I'll keep an eye on him." Tiny set his hoe down against the side of the dike and clambered out of the field, his bare feet flashing as he raced after my brother.

By now other people were leaving their fields to join the crowd at the front of the valley.

Foxfire came dashing back a moment later. He looked around excitedly, aware that everyone was watching him. "Harmony's come back," he announced. There was a thump as Peony dropped her basket. Foxfire turned to her at the same time the rest of us did. "He's all in rags and bony as a skeleton," he added.

I snaked my hand around Foxfire's ankle and toppled him from the dike into our field. "I wish you'd use as much energy farming as you do talking."

Foxfire got up indignantly. "I'm all dirty now."

"It shows you're getting close to your work." I pointed to his hoe. "Now pick that up and get back in this field."

Peony looked a bit flustered when she stared down at the weeds in her basket. "This won't be much of a welcome-home feast."

I knew she was playing the helpless little girl again because it usually got her what she wanted. For a moment I thought about sending her off to try her act on someone else; but then I told myself she probably couldn't help it. Acting out that role was as natural to her as breathing. I found myself thinking of what I would want if our positions were reversed.

"Well," I sighed, "I can give you two squash, and I'll talk to the other women on the lane to see what they have to spare. I guess for an occasion like this, we can all go a little hungrier tonight."

"Are the squash big ones?" Peony wondered.

I shut my eyes and said a prayer. Surely I must have been working off a load of sins today. "They'll be big enough."

"Good," Peony said, and without even thanking me, she started to walk briskly over the dike tops toward the crowd.

"Why do I give in to her all the time?" I complained to Aster.

"Because you've got such a big heart." Foxfire got back up on top of the dike and dusted himself off.

"And where are you going?" I demanded. I reached out with the hoe to hook his leg, but he eluded me with a nimble hop.

"Harmony's going to tell us all about his travels." Foxfire began to back down the dike top. "He's heard all sorts of stories about the demon lands overseas."

I opened my mouth to shout something after him, but Aster merely chuckled. "You might as well save your breath. He's gone for the day." She glanced at Tiny's hoe. "And so is my husband."

"Why did Heaven give men such strong backs and such weak minds if they hate to work?" I grumbled.

Aster shrugged and went back to her hoeing. "You forget that Heaven also gave them sisters and wives."

Chapter Twelve

Everyone talked to Harmony about the job prospects outside the valley, and the news was bad. He said there were a hundred men competing for every job—even up in the new demon city that was being built. But of course Foxfire didn't bother with anything practical. Oh, no, he had to ask about what stories his cousin had heard.

He was full of the news when he and Father came home later that evening for supper. Harmony had told him a story about a golden mountain overseas in a demon land known as America. At the foot of the golden mountain was a strange city of tents, like the ten villages of the nomads of the north. The demons themselves had heads that were on fire and spoke with stonelike tongues. (Father added that while it was true the demons had hair in different colors—including yellow—their tongues were nimble enough when they cared to learn our language.)

According to Harmony, the mountain was higher than the strongest hawk could fly over and so wide that the fleetest horse needed a week to ride around its base. When the sun shone, the mountain was so bright that men and demons alike were blinded. They could go outside only in the twilight, and then everyone scurried about picking up nuggets and stuffing them into sacks as fast as they could.

It was just like Foxfire to believe a wild story like that. "It all sounds like rubbish to me."

The blood rushed to Foxfire's face. "But there's a golden mountain in the serpent story."

"That's just some poet's fancy name for a temple. It doesn't mean a thing." But I couldn't help looking toward the carvings of the window lattice. The silver moonlight gave a soft, fleshlike glow to the wooden serpent-woman and her marsh monsters as they glared at the temple on its tall mountain.

"You don't see a wagging tail unless there's a dog to go with it." He held his bowl out for a refill.

[123]

"The meal's finished," I said, guarding the cooked rice on the stove.

Foxfire set down his empty bowl. "Is that really all?" His finger idly picked up a grain of rice and set it on his tongue.

I shrugged my shoulders in embarrassment—it was my fault that I hadn't managed things better. "You saw what the Phoenixes did to our crops," I reminded him. "And on top of that, I had to give something to Peony."

Father clicked his chopsticks unhappily over his own bowl. "How bad is the damage?"

I couldn't remember things ever being this bad when Mother was in charge; and it made me feel like a fool—a clown who only made other people laugh when I tried to imitate Mother. "Pretty bad. We'll have to buy our own food for the next month."

Father rested his chin against his chest for a moment and then shrugged. "We could sell some of this old furniture. I hear there's a clerk coming here from town to buy stuff. I'll have him come over." Otherwise we would've had to carry our things into town piece by piece until we'd sold it all.

Foxfire shoved his empty bowl away. "But we'd be all right if you let me go to the land of the golden mountain." He spoke so matter-of-factly, you might have thought he was talking about crossing the lane.

But before either Father or I could say anything, we heard a *tap-tap-tap* at the door. We all held our breaths. It had been years since we had last heard that knock.

Tap-tap-tap.

It was a soft enough sound, but it roused Father more than the beating of a drum or a gong. And it cheered him up better than any banquet or tonic could have. "Cassia," he ordered, "put out the candle. Foxfire, get the shutter. He won't want his face being seen."

I ran to snuff out the candle. Foxfire went over to the window and reached through the lattice to knock away the long stick we used to prop up the shutter.

Though Father tried, his bad leg kept him from moving very fast. When he was finally in place by the door, he nodded his head to me. I snuffed out the candle. Father jerked the door open. A tall silhouette stood there. "Banish the darkness," he murmured.

"Restore the light," Father whispered back in response.

The man slipped inside and Father closed the door again. When I lit the candle, I saw it was Cousin

Spider after all these years. His shirt was more tattered and his large straw hat more battered and his hair was already prematurely gray, but he still had the same quick smile.

Spider immediately threw his arms around Father. "It's good to see you."

Father returned the hug, squeezing his eyes shut with joy and holding on as tightly as a drowning man would hold on to his rescuer. "It's been five years since you last came by. I was beginning to think you'd all forgotten about me."

Cousin Spider slapped Father on the back. "Forget the man who fought beside me at Three Powers?"

Father stepped back, his hand chopping rhythmically at the air as he sang,

> "Oh, didn't we have fun, boys?
> Didn't we have fun?"

Cousin Spider swung his arm enthusiastically in time to the tune as he joined in.

> "We made the demons turn their tails,
> And didn't we make them run?"

Then they both were laughing and hugging one another again. When Spider finally swung around, he caught sight of Foxfire first. "Is this your boy?

How he's grown!" And he twisted round again. "But where's your oldest? Where's my sweetheart?" He was surprised when he saw me. "She's a woman now."

"Thank you," I said, pleased.

"It's time to think of marrying you off." He stroked the stubble on his chin. "In fact, I know a man on the coast who has a nice boy." He glanced over at Father. "They're both in the Brotherhood, and the boy has a little learning too."

"A clerk?" Father limped over to the table.

"No, a fisherman." Spider kept pace slowly beside him.

I went over to the stove and dished out a bowl of rice. Foxfire and I would go even hungrier tomorrow; but that couldn't be helped. Feeding Spider came first. "I can't swim," I said, scowling.

"He's not suggesting you for one of the crew, just a wife," Father said to me, but he squeezed Spider's arm. "But unless the boy is ready for a tigress from the hills, you'd better pass on her."

"Yes, I suppose we should concentrate on one war at a time." Spider reached a hand into his pouch and pulled out two large pieces of candy. "I suppose you're too old for these now?"

I licked my lips. I hadn't had any sweets since his

last visit. Hurriedly, I put a few vegetables on top of the rice bowl and brought it over to the table where Foxfire was already hovering. Neither of us wanted to be the first to grab the candy; and yet neither of us could take our eyes off it.

"You're never really too old for sweets, are you?" I asked.

Spider took the bowl from me with a nod of thanks. "No, I guess you aren't," he said kindly.

I snatched up the larger one and popped it into my mouth—and savored the delicious sweetness.

"Now you look like my Cassia." Spider tweaked one of my pigtails as Foxfire popped the other piece into his mouth. We each chewed blissfully for a few moments while Father sat down.

"Your parents are all right."

"I have no parents, remember?" Spider bent his head and shoveled some rice into his mouth. "You're my family now."

Father rubbed the top of the table while he hunted for something else to say. In the meantime, though, Foxfire edged in closer to the table. "Cousin, you wander around a lot. Have you heard of a golden mountain overseas?" His words came out thickly since the lump of candy was still on his tongue.

Spider straddled the bench. "Why?"

Foxfire's tongue shoved the candy over against his cheek, making a lump there. "But if there is a golden mountain, don't you think it would be wonderful to see it?"

"It's the talk of the province. But I wouldn't be in any hurry to leave." Spider gazed around the softly lit room as if he were storing away each object in his memory like some golden treasure. "There's many a time when I was tumbling around in the dark or hiding in a cave that I wished I could be back in Three Willows."

"We must restore the light," Father scolded him gently.

Spider planted a hand on either knee. "I wish the Brotherhood had a half dozen as dedicated as you. We'd have the Work done in no time." He started to talk about the time they had marched off to Canton. The memories flowed as heady as brandy that's been distilled and then distilled again until it is an almost purifying fire. I busied myself at the stove. I could see that Father was sitting up straighter and easier—as if he had just thrown off eight long, weary years.

I'd finished my candy by the time I brought a cup of tea over to Spider; Foxfire—being slower and more methodical—still had his. He made a point of opening his mouth to show me there was still a bit left on his tongue. I shrugged one shoulder at him as I set the tea before Spider.

He nodded his head at me in thanks and gave a large sigh. "I miss you, cousin." Spider seemed surprised when I didn't bring Father a cup of tea too. He glanced over at me and saw that I had settled with my back against a wall.

"I've already drunk too much tea," Father hurried to explain, and then raised both his palms slightly. "Please. Don't wait for me." We had only a little tea left, so we saved it for special occasions. But of course it was too embarrassing for Father to admit that. It was a white lie that fooled no one, but it did save Father some face.

"May the darkness vanish soon." Spider lifted his cup in a toast and then sipped it.

"You know"—Father leaned forward on his elbows—"the road might seem smoother and shorter if you had a brother to keep your spirits up."

I gave a start and straightened up. It hadn't occurred to me that after this morning's humiliation, Father might want to run away almost as much as Foxfire did. Sometimes they were more alike than either wanted to admit. Mother had been right about that.

Setting down his cup, Spider kept on talking as he wolfed down his food. "Believe me, you wouldn't want to go on this mission if you knew what it was. I almost hope I fail."

Father picked up a piece of rice straw from the floor. "I couldn't leave the village with things being the way they are anyway."

"Hard times?" Spider peered at Father over the rim of his rice bowl.

"And likely to get harder. The Phoenixes have made it impossible for us ever since one of them bought a scholarly title." He gave a bitter laugh. "They say the man can barely sign his name."

Spider grunted. "Sometimes you don't even have to do that much if you click enough money in front of the officials."

In ancient, more honest times, a man could only earn the title of scholar after years of long study and passing three exams, each one harder than the last one. However, owning even the lowest scholarly title—whether earned or bought—gave the holder and his clan certain advantages. For one thing, unscrupulous people like the Phoenixes could use the title to get out of certain kinds of taxes; but more importantly, it made it easier for the Phoenixes to see the government officials who were "brother" scholars. It made it easier to pass along bribes, so the Phoenixes usually had their way on almost everything.

Spider set down his empty rice bowl. "They'll have their day of reckoning, and then they'll be sorry."

Father's fingers made another loop in the long piece of straw. "Well, it better come soon. They've also hired Dusty."

Spider picked a bit of tea leaf from the rim of his cup. "I'd heard that Dusty had gone bad and left the Brotherhood."

"You don't know how bad." Father quickly described this morning's raid. "I did what I could, but . . ." Father's voice died off.

Spider stared at Father for a long time—he could guess at just how badly Dusty had treated Father. "I'll see what the Brotherhood can do." He finished his tea in a gulp. "But losses were heavy six years ago when the uprising failed. We all had to lie low while the Manchus and their puppets were hunting us."

Father jerked the loop hard so it slid into a small, tight knot. "I felt bad that I couldn't be there to share your troubles."

"Yes, I know," Spider said. He spoke with Father a little longer, reliving missions years ago and recalling many comrades—most of whom seemed to be dead. Finally, he slapped his hand on the table and stood up slowly—as if reluctant to go. "I know things seem terrible," he said, "but you really are better off here."

"Things are that bad for the Brotherhood?" Father asked.

"For myself *and* the Brotherhood." Spider gave a clumsy pat to Father's shoulder and started for the door.

Father was quiet as he shut the door behind Spider; and when I relit the candle, I could see how sad he was. But Foxfire started to crow right away. "You see, there really is a golden mountain overseas."

But Spider's visit had renewed Father's faith in the Work, so he glared at Foxfire now as if Foxfire had just spat on his shoe. "How can you think about going over there? Look at how the demons are poisoning our country with their drugs." He gestured toward his bad leg. "And look at what they've done to me."

Foxfire, though, didn't want to give up on his dream. "America is a different country from England; but even if they were the same, surely all demons aren't bad."

"The only good thing about the demons are their guns," Father insisted. "We must reject everything else. Only if we modernize our armies with their guns can we hope to drive them away from our land." Father seemed to be recovering some of his old pride and dignity.

"How many guns would it take?" Foxfire tried to argue. "And how could we ever get that many?"

Father poked his finger at the air. "That's where I've got you. It wouldn't take as many as you think. I've heard their hunters use a certain type of gun when they hunt waterfowl near Canton. It's only good for a short range, but it scatters pellets over a wide area. And it has ammunition that can kill humans just as easily. They call it a *shotgun*." Father emphasized the last, strange-sounding word with a nod of his head. "If I'd had one of those, I could have chased Dusty out of the whole district."

"But would the demons sell them to us?" I wondered.

Father sat down confidently on a chair. "If the price was right, the demons would sell anything."

Foxfire spread out his hands. "Maybe we could learn more from the demons than better ways of killing. The path to our future may begin overseas."

Father shook his head firmly. "Have you taken

[134]

leave of your senses?" He tapped his fingers against the table. "Here. In this land of your ancestors—that's where your future lies."

"But—" Foxfire began.

"I don't want to hear any more about it." Father reared his head up sternly. "I may not be the fighter I once was, but I'm still the head of this household."

I looked at Father in dismay. Though he was well within his rights, it didn't do any good just to tell my stubborn, imaginative brother to shut up. The best way to deal with Foxfire was Mother's method: Let him get the talk out of his system, knocking down his points one by one—as I had with his wild notions about seed selection.

Yet I couldn't blame Father, because I didn't always have the patience to do that either. But I wished Father had taken some time right at that moment. As it was, he had only managed to fix the golden mountain in Foxfire's mind as a real goal that he could reach someday.

Chapter Thirteen

I watched in alarm as the golden mountain seemed to grow within Foxfire's mind over the next few days. He became more and more addicted to the dream of a fabulous mountain of gold in the same way some people were drawn to opium. So I should have known he was up to something when the clerk came from Fortunate Enterprises to buy furniture.

With the clerk had come over two dozen coolies to carry away his purchases. As soon as he saw them, Foxfire disappeared inside our house. When I followed him into there, I found my brother dipping a rice bowl into the jar of water I kept in the kitchen.

"What are you doing?" I demanded from the doorway. The water was being strictly rationed now.

He straightened guiltily, setting the cover back on the jar. "I thought the coolies might be thirsty. I was just going to give each of them a sip." He shrugged. "You can take it from my share if you like."

If anything, the men from the town were even bonier and more ragged than we were. If Harmony's tales were true, they didn't even have homes, but slept in alleys and doorways like stray dogs. Perhaps they had even fought with one another for a day's work, even if it was only for a few cash—the round copper coins with the square holes through their centers.

Ashamed, I ran my fingertips along my cheeks. They would probably have to work the entire day without a drop of water. How could I say I cared about the Work when I thought only of myself? Sometimes my little brother was a better revolutionary than I was. "No, we'll take it from both our shares."

Even Mother would have had a hard time finding something good to say about the clerk. He was a haughty little man in a merchant's gown and vest. He kept the gown raised slightly between his fingertips so that the hem would not get dirty. When he spoke, it was in the dialect of the Three Districts, which are up around Canton. They say that the people from the area could charm the hams off a pig; but not this one.

The only thing he bought in the Golden Cat's house was a four-poster bed that the coolies had to dismantle and carry out. I wished they'd carried it out assembled, because it was supposed to be a wonder. I don't know what agonies the Golden Cat had gone through before he had decided to part with it. But even he was hurting for money like the rest of us.

The clerk went through the rest of the village briskly, hardly doing more than glancing at items people wanted to show him. It turned out he was looking for old pieces—antiques that rich collectors would purchase—not ordinary furniture. That meant most families would have to bring their furniture into town and try to sell it themselves.

When he did make a deal, it was always after some sharp bargaining. Then his coolies would carry out some family's prized possession: a chair carved by someone's great-grandfather from valuable hardwood, or maybe a bronze urn. The items would appear bobbing up and down on the backs of his workers as if on a human stream washing the memories of the clan out into the street.

When he came to our house, I raised the shutter, propping it open with a stick so that he could see better. But instead of looking at the table and benches, the clerk stared down at his feet, where the silhouettes of strange marsh monsters twined and writhed as if alive. "What's this?" He turned, his eyebrows drawing together intently.

"It's only an old thing my wife brought with her." Father tried to draw his attention to what we wished to sell. "These fine pieces are what we wanted to show you."

But the clerk only had eyes for Mother's story window. His head jerked this way and that like a small bird as he studied it. "A bit crude perhaps, but the carver knew what he wanted to say—and wasn't afraid to say it. I have an acquaintance with a taste for curiosity pieces. He might be willing to pay a little something for it."

"It's not for sale," Father said firmly. "We thought you might want a strong table and benches."

The clerk merely glanced at them, dragging his fingers across the tops, which I had cleaned so meticulously. "No, no, it's all too plain and ordinary."

[139]

"It's served the family all these years. It would serve someone else just as well." He tested the table legs. "Just feel how sturdy these are. You could kill and flay a water buffalo on top of this and not break it."

The little man tapped his fingertips together. "No doubt, but few of our clientele have such hobbies." He started to turn toward the door brusquely. "So if that's all you have—" He stopped when he saw Mother's other things. "Now that chest is interesting. Hmm. And a wardrobe too."

"It belonged to her mother." Father stepped in front of the clerk, blocking his view.

"You mean it's not for sale either?" The clerk clicked his tongue impatiently.

"They're old, but you get used to having certain things around." Actually, they had a good deal of sentimental value. However, politeness insisted that Father be modest about such things. "But the table—"

The clerk pivoted. "Yes, it's quite a nice table. I'm sure someone else will be glad to buy it." He grasped the hem of his robe so that it wouldn't brush the wall near the stove. Generations of cooking fires had left it rather sooty. "Thank you so kindly for showing me your charming little house. Now if you'll excuse me, I have some other houses to inspect."

"Wait," I said. "Perhaps it's time to think about getting some new things." I patted the table. "We might sell the chest and wardrobe if you bought the table and the benches and a few other things."

"But the table and benches are so big. It would take four of my men to carry them." The clerk licked his lips, but his mind seemed to be calculating. "However, if you're thinking of getting rid of such old things, perhaps you'd think of parting with the window as well." He pointed toward the lattice.

I was truly torn between the two choices. As long as the window filled our house with its shadows, Mother's stories would live and so would Mother; yet we badly needed cash for seed and food. I felt like I had to choose between abandoning that last little part of Mother we owned and starving to death.

But Father came to my rescue. "No, not the window. Just the chest and wardrobe."

"I'll have to think on it. Perhaps after I've seen a few other houses, I'll have a better sense of how many men I have to spare." He began to walk toward the doorway.

But I'd seen a certain glint in his eye when he had been looking at them, so I decided to call his bluff. "We might be out," I warned him.

He paused in mid step. "Oh?" He swung around again. "What a shame."

I ran a hand down the face of the wardrobe over the ornate carvings. "It's a woodworking style you don't see in this area."

"If I may be so bold, your mother was from . . . ?" He pressed a fingertip against his lips.

"The marshlands to the west," I said.

The clerk dropped his hand. "Ah, how unfortunate. It's a style that doesn't always sell well."

"Perhaps it's so rare in this area that people don't know how to value it." I named a price that was double the amount we needed.

"But that means there's a certain risk buying something for which there isn't a market." He studied me from the corners of his eyes.

I knew I had him hooked now. "I think it could find admirers."

We discussed the matter for a little while longer before the clerk finally heaved a huge, elaborate sigh. "Well, I like you people, so I'll buy your things without the window." I silently thanked my mother's father for the love and skill he had put into his carving; but then the clerk added, "Provided you make me a promise."

"What's that?" Father asked suspiciously.

The clerk smoothed the front of his embroidered silk vest. "When the time comes to sell the window, you'll come to me first."

"We'll never sell the window." Father stepped in protectively between the clerk and it.

The clerk simply smiled—as if he knew better. "Yes, of course," he said quickly. Then we got down to some serious haggling, settling upon a price that the clerk announced would ruin his master and that we said would make us starve—though it would actually let us plant our rice crop and have some money left over to feed ourselves.

While I hated to sell Mother's other things, I reminded myself of the plants we would grow with the seed and the stomachs we would fill with food. Her furniture was going in a good cause, after all.

We didn't have much, so it didn't take me very long to clear our things out of the chest and the wardrobe while the clerk counted out the cash into Father's hand. Then, when the clerk called to his men, a half dozen of them came into courtyard, and Foxfire tagged along after them.

"No, the mountain's really there," one of the coolies was saying. His ribs stood out so much that he seemed more bone than skin.

And I'd thought Foxfire had been giving them

water out of the goodness of his heart! Instead, he'd dipped into our precious supplies to bribe them for more information on that mountain of his.

"I've a friend who went," a second man said. He was even more of a skeleton than the first one. "The merchants have it all worked out, you see. They've bought him his ticket, and once he's over there, my friend will work off his debt gradually. But he'll still be able to send money home."

The first coolie nudged the second with a bony elbow. It was hard to believe that either of them could lift anything in their emaciated state; but I'd seen their fellow workers do just that—even those who were even thinner than this pair. "Tell him how your friend had to guarantee he'd pay back the money."

"Well"—the second man rubbed his side—"normally you'd put up your house and fields as security, or you'd get some rich relative to promise to repay the money. But they had nothing and no one else, so his wife put herself up as his bond. If he doesn't repay the money, she'll be claimed as a slave."

"Your friend's a fool, if you ask me," the first coolie snorted. "What if something happens to him during the voyage? Or if he dies once he's over there?"

The second man looked at the first as if he were

an idiot. "What do you think would've happened if he had stayed here? He couldn't feed both of them. She would have wound up being sold to some brothel anyway."

Grasping the rim of the bowl, Foxfire banged it against his leg. "But what's she living on in the meantime?"

"Oh, they've thought of that too. You get a little money in advance so your family can survive until the remittances start coming."

I stalked toward my infuriating brother. "And I suppose you repay the entire sum at high interest rates."

"That's right." The second man nodded to me.

"It sounds like a cheap and easy way to collect slaves." I sniffed. "I notice you didn't go with your friend."

"I'm not that desperate yet," the second coolie had to admit. "The trip's no pleasure cruise. They cram as many men as they can into the hold of a ship. Some men get sick and die; or fights break out because you're all crowded together, and more people die."

The first coolie chimed in. "They say on some ships one out of every three men dies. The odds are better juggling daggers."

The clerk beckoned to them from the doorway. "Hey, I'm not paying you fools to chat."

The first coolie slapped Foxfire on the shoulder. "Thanks for the water. And good luck."

"Good luck to you, too." Foxfire said to them.

I snatched the bowl from his hand, resisting the urge to break it over his thick skull. I don't think Mother knew what she was asking when she told me to take care of my fool of a brother. "Honestly, I can't leave you alone for one moment."

Foxfire planted his fists on his hips. "I think the only way I could get away from your nagging would be to put an ocean between us. Did you ever stop to think that my dreams might not be the same as yours?"

"You're too clever for your own good," I scolded him. "You're always chasing after some wild scheme— the wilder the better. You'd just get yourself hurt— or worse."

"You're always being so practical," Foxfire complained. "Don't you ever have any dreams, Cassia?"

All the frustrations and fears seemed to explode within me like a string of little firecrackers exploding all at once. "Don't you think I'd like to? Do you think I enjoy scolding you all the time? But one of

[146]

us has to be realistic about things. It's what Mother told me to do."

Before Foxfire could say anything else, the clerk came outside.

"Now remember," the clerk said to Father. "I get first crack at that window."

"You'll be waiting a long time." Father dangled the strings of cash from his hand.

The clerk looked up at the sky, which was empty of any clouds. "I'll take that chance," he said confidently, as if he knew he would see Father—and soon. "Farmers are all optimists."

I glanced at Foxfire and saw the absent look on his face—as if he were already boarding the ship to go overseas. It seemed he thought the same thing as the clerk.

Chapter Fourteen

That autumn's harvest was the worst that anyone could remember. Though Foxfire and I practically broke our backs weeding and hand watering the second rice crop, the yields were so small that we wound up giving all we had to the Golden Cat. I didn't know where we would get the seed for our winter vegetables.

But I didn't let myself worry about that. Most of my mind was taken up with getting through the day. As I gathered weeds and ferns, it was maddening to think of the rice we had grown but were unable to keep.

I was standing at the stove inside our house when

Father returned from one of his patrols. He walked over and smiled a silent greeting as I went on stirring the soup boiling in the wok.

He sniffed the odd-smelling steam rising from it. "What's that delicious smell?" he asked.

"Weed soup." In my embarrassment I banged the lid down on the wok. Up to now I'd always prided myself on serving meals just as good as Mother's. "At least it might fool our stomachs for a while." Only the poorest families tried to eat grass soup, because it was a slow form of starvation.

Father turned me around so I could see the shadows of Mother's story window. The sun was just setting, making them stretch farther into the room as if each creature were growing as large as life. He pointed at one particular shadow. "It doesn't seem to have hurt that horse any." Actually, it was a creature with the body of a crab and the head of a horse.

"I wish he could have the soup and we could have him." I smacked my lips at the thought. Father and I teased one another, selecting various monsters for our imaginary banquet. By the time we were finished, I felt lighter in my heart. It was just the sort of thing Mother would have done to keep our spirits up. Finally, as my eyes followed the sweeping curves of the serpent-woman, I smiled at Father. "You know, I almost feel like Mother's going to walk through the doorway in a moment and begin one of her stories."

Father nodded his head understandingly. "She had a story for every creature in that lattice. I almost feel like they're kin."

Feeling better, I got down the bowls from a shelf. "We can serve the soup as soon as Foxfire gets back."

"How do you know when it's done?" Father handed some plates to me.

I set them down on top of the stove. "Oh, weed soup is ready quick enough. It just takes a while to work up the nerve to serve it."

Father was outside in the courtyard washing up when I heard Foxfire slam the gates shut. "What're you doing, Father?" Foxfire tried to joke. "Making soup?"

"There's so much dust in the air that I think you would've eaten enough of it already." Father came in, using his shirt to wipe off his shoulders and chest. "Foxfire's back." He sat down on the floor at about the same spot where he would have been if we'd had a table.

"Yes, I heard a sample of his humor. Let's see if he can keep on joking when he sees his meal." I began pouring the soup into the bowls, and on each plate put a portion of the one remaining sweet potato, which I had baked in the stove's fire.

When I brought the plate and bowl over to Father, he took his spoon from his plate and picked up his slice of sweet potato. "I'll take a smaller piece."

"There's plenty for all," I lied.

However, Father added his share to Foxfire's plate.

"That was the one bit of real food," I complained.

"But it's all so tasty." Father stuffed a spoonful of weeds bravely into his mouth and proceeded to chew it with immense enthusiasm.

I couldn't help laughing at the sight. "You look just like a water buffalo."

Father swallowed and held a warning finger up to his lips. "Not so loud, or someone might take steaks from me."

"I hope it never comes to that"—I sighed—"but you do hear stories about what some people do in a famine."

Suddenly Foxfire stormed into the house—as if something outside had upset him. But he didn't talk right away about what was bothering him. Instead he spoke about it indirectly.

"You know"—he plopped down in front of his soup bowl—"I spoke to some of the coolies who took away our furniture. They say that there really is a golden mountain." And he described the system where a ticket would be advanced on credit.

"Yes, yes. I've heard plenty of fairy tales like that." Father lifted a spoonful of weeds and blew on it. "And at the end, everyone goes up to a place in the clouds."

"I thought that was supposed to happen after the Revolution," Foxfire grumbled as he folded his legs into a lotus position.

"It will come one day, young man. Mark my words." Father thrust the spoonful into his mouth and began to eat the weeds methodically.

"Of course it will, Father." I gave a slight shake of my head toward Foxfire as a signal to keep quiet—but he ignored me.

It was as if he had to get the words out before something dreadful happened to him—as if he were straw that had been set on fire. "So what would happen if your Revolution came tomorrow? We'd still have the same rents and taxes to pay."

I bristled at him. "But things will be done fairly once we've gotten rid of the Manchus."

He planted a hand on either knee. "But don't you see? It's not the Manchu dynasty that's our real enemy. And it's not the demons and their opium. It's poverty." He began to tick off the items on his fingers. "If it isn't a drought, then sometimes it's a flood that ruins the crops. Or it's some disease that wipes out the plants, or a horde of insects, or maybe it's taxes to pay for some new war, or it's bandits." He slapped his hands back down on his knees for emphasis. "We can expect one year out of every three to be a bad one."

I slipped the broad, heavy, spoonlike spatula around in the wok. "It's something farmers have to live with."

"Or they don't live at all." There was a hard, relentless edge to his voice that I'd never heard before. "We don't even know what we're going to eat tomorrow."

I banged the spatula angrily on the side of the wok. "I'd like to see you do better."

Frustrated, Foxfire flapped his knees against the floor. "I'm not blaming you, Cassia. It's just that we don't have to go through all this misery. I could go overseas and find work and then send money home to you."

Before Father or I could answer, we heard a child begin wailing outside, and then a second and third joined in. "What's that?" Putting the spatula down, I started toward the front door.

"Cassia." Foxfire grabbed my hand, but he wouldn't look at me. "It would be kinder if you didn't go."

"What's happening?" Father demanded.

Foxfire wouldn't look at Father either but stared straight ahead. "While I was washing up in the courtyard, I overheard them talking in the lane. Harmony is going to take Peony into town and sell her." And I finally understood what had gotten into Foxfire—he'd been scared for all of us, but especially for me.

I didn't love Peony, but I wouldn't have wished that fate on my worst enemy. "Oh, no." I pulled free of Foxfire's hold.

"Cassia." Father almost barked at me. When I turned around, he motioned me back toward him. "For once, I have to agree with your brother. It would be kinder if you weren't there as a witness. It would only add to their grief."

I clenched my hands into fists and stood swaying over Father. "But why would Harmony do that? I thought he loved her."

"That's why he's selling her." Foxfire looked unhappily down at his bowl. "He says the brothel will feed her well. And the money will keep the rest of them alive until the winter vegetable crop."

I put my fingers over my mouth as I realized

something. "She's only a few months older than I am."

"Yes." Father shoved his plate and bowl away from him as if he had suddenly lost his appetite.

"They've been trying to live on weed soup," I murmured through my hand.

"It doesn't sustain you for long." Foxfire leaned forward urgently. "We could starve to death in less than a month."

"How can you even think of deserting our land?" Father set his bowl down.

"I think it's the other way around," Foxfire argued. "It's the land that's deserted us. The earth is tired and worn out. Look how much fertilizer it takes now to get a decent crop."

"Enough." Father slammed a fist on the floor. Foxfire looked frightened—as if he suspected just how far he had overstepped himself. Both of us held our breaths wondering what Father might do next. "Neither of you will ever be slaves."

He shoved himself to his feet. "Your mother would want me to do this." Going to the stove, he picked up the spatula.

I gave Father a puzzled look. "What are you going to do?"

Father gripped the spatula as if it were a sword

and marched toward the window. "We can't afford to be sentimental anymore."

I clutched at Father's arm. "Not Mother's window. It's where she used to tell all her stories."

A muscle worked on Father's cheek while he stared down at the hand that was holding him. "Your mother," he said gently, "would have been the last person to value a window more than her children. She used to say that you were our future."

My hand dropped woodenly to my side. "But all the good things are being taken away from us."

Father stood there for a moment as if he had to work up his nerve. "The important thing is that you live to carry on the Work." Raising the spatula, he jabbed at the wall surrounding the window lattice. Little bits of plaster began pattering down like dry, dead raindrops.

For a long time I simply listened to Father stab at the wall. And then, much to my shame, the breath seemed to explode from my lungs in loud sobs and the tears began falling. I felt as if Mother were dying all over again.

Foxfire squirmed over to me. "I swear that I never expected Father to do this."

I know that I had promised Mother to take care of him, but my brother had been so stupid and callous that I couldn't bear it anymore. "It's all your fault. You egged Father on with all that stupid talk about the golden mountain."

"I still think it's the only way out for us," he said, and then gave a slow shake of his head. "But I'm not going to fight you. The last thing Father needs to hear right now is another quarrel."

"Yes." Father paused and wiped the sweat from his forehead. "Don't spoil the sacrifice with bickering." Then, taking a deep breath, he jammed the spatula into the wall and began to lever the lattice away from it. The wood of the lattice—so lovingly carved and polished—began to creak in protest, as if it didn't want to leave.

"No, please, don't do that," I begged. "I just didn't look hard enough in the hills. I'll go out early tomorrow—"

With one last, determined jerk, Father forced the lattice from the window hole. Dropping the spatula with a clatter to the floor, he hugged the lattice carefully against his chest. "There are all kinds of wars we have to fight. Sometimes it's against the Manchus; sometimes it's against the demons. Sometimes it's even against ourselves. Right now we have to make this sacrifice in order to survive."

I sat back slowly upon my heels. Mother had

always valued two things most in the world: the family and the Work. That was why she had told me to watch out for my father and brother. Suddenly I knew as certainly as if Mother were whispering it in my ear that she would have sold a dozen story windows if it meant we could live to carry on the Work. So for her sake I had to forgive them.

I tried to keep my voice as strong and controlled as a warrior's. "You're right, of course," I said to Father.

But the large hole in our wall seemed like a great gaping wound in our home; and all the warm, loving memories of my childhood were flowing through it and out into the twilight, never to be replaced.

Chapter Fifteen

Despite the sacrifice, we didn't get to enjoy more than a few meals before things got worse. It was only a few evenings later that we heard the *tap-tap-tap* at the door.

"So soon?" Father got to his feet eagerly and limped toward the door as if he could already see the banners being raised, the drums and gongs beginning to sound the march. I got ready by the candle while Foxfire went over to the window from sheer habit. But of course this time it was covered by a tattered shirt through which he couldn't reach. But he could peer through one of the holes. "It looks like we've got more than one visitor."

"Maybe it's time to finish the Work." Father stood by the door, waiting impatiently for me to blow out the candle. When it was out, Father yanked the door open.

"Banish the darkness." Spider used a normal tone of voice.

"Restore the light," Father answered loudly.

"I'm not hiding my face any longer," Spider called from the doorway. "Light the candle, Cassia."

When I had done so, I could see that Father was excited as a small boy at a New Year's feast. "Then the day really has come." He plucked at the red cloth wrapped around Spider's arm.

"No, not yet. But almost." Spider waved a hand behind him. "Come in, boys, and meet your older brother."

Father stepped back as a half dozen ragged, unkempt men swaggered into the house with sacks over their shoulders. They also wore armbands to match Spider's.

Father stared at them and then protested to Spider, "They look more like bandits than revolutionaries."

There were sharp, angry looks from the others, but Spider held up his index finger in warning—like some schoolteacher. "One-Eye's an outlaw, not a bandit. Bandits are only thieves, but an outlaw is someone who's been hounded so much by the government that he's driven to steal. How else do you expect him to survive?"

Father flung out his hand contemptuously. "One-Eye cares no more about political persecution than a duck. He only wants a chance to loot."

Spider gave a stern cough. "His goals match ours at the moment. We need troops who know this territory. It's the quickest and most effective way of replacing our losses."

Father turned to Spider in disbelief. "You can't mean to use these pigs to do the Work?"

One of the bandits jerked a knife from his sash and took a step forward, but Spider tripped him neatly. Placing a foot on the man's wrist, Spider snapped, "Remember what One-Eye said would happen to anyone who disobeyed me."

The man paled underneath his coating of dirt. One-Eye was notorious for the imaginative way he tortured the people he disliked. The man dropped the knife. "He just shouldn't insult us. What kind of sworn brother says that to another?"

Spider let go of the man. The man grabbed his knife and scrambled back to his feet. "He's right, you know," Spider said to Father. "You ought to apologize. We must have discipline in the Work. That applies not only to them but to both of us as well." When Father simply glared, Spider added in a tired, sad voice, "We all have to follow orders like good soldiers."

There was something in the resigned way he acted that made me wonder if he had really wanted to recruit One-Eye. Father must have picked up on Cousin Spider's tone too. "Yes, well," he mumbled, "I'm sorry if I spoke ill of a brother." But he refused to look at the bandits when he spoke.

"There now." Spider clapped his hands together nervously. "We're all one big, happy family, so I know you won't mind sharing your food with your new brothers."

"We don't have much, but we'll give you what we can. It's the Phoenixes who have more," Father suggested.

Spider tugged at his ear uncomfortably. "Yes, I intend to deal with them later—after our new brothers have had some training." It was a face-saving way of saying that he was scared of the Phoenixes.

Father sucked in his breath. "I see. The Phoenixes have Dusty to defend them, but the Youngs only have a cripple."

"We're asking for contributions to a worthy enough cause, after all." Spider's voice had taken on a warning edge. "I came here first because I thought you'd set a good example."

"I see where it is." The bandit with the knife started to head for the baskets where we had our rice stored.

Father blocked his way. "I said we'd give you what we could."

Spider hooked Father's arm and jerked him against the wall. "Don't worry. We're only taking half."

"Half?" Father tried to pull away from Spider's grasp. "But we'll starve."

"We decided on half of each household's food. I can't make any exceptions. Not yours. Not . . . not Windy's." Spider kept a tight grip on Father's arm. "We need extra supplies if we're going to recruit more men."

"Contributions to the cause," Foxfire said disgustedly to Spider. "Taxes or donations, officials or rebels, it's always the poor farmer who has to pay for all that high-flown talk."

With a frantic burst of strength, Father pulled free from Spider and stumbled against the stove. The heavy kitchen cleaver was there near his hand. Desperately, he grasped the hilt. "My wife and I didn't give up everything for something like this. Get out of our house."

Frightened, Foxfire walked toward Father. "Let's just give them whatever they want so we can get rid of them."

I looked at Foxfire contemptuously. He was being as much of a coward as he had been with Dusty; but Father scolded my brother before I could. "I might have expected that kind of talk from you. How can we hope to keep the Work pure if we aren't?"

"Don't you understand?" Spider's eyes pleaded with Father silently. "Our country's dying. If we don't drive out the Manchus soon, we'll be too weak to defend ourselves against the demons. They want to chop us up like a roast duck and gobble us down. We have no choice but to make some compromises with our principles."

Father shook his head recklessly. "You can't expect people to follow you when you behave like this." And there was a strange, hungry look to his face as if he hadn't eaten in days; but he was staring not at any food but at Spider.

Foxfire grabbed Father's arm so he couldn't wield the cleaver. "Father, don't. We've sacrificed enough for the Work."

"Get away from me." Father twisted, trying to elbow Foxfire to the side: but that was all the distraction Spider's men needed. The bandits fell on Father and Foxfire so that they tumbled to the floor under a swarm of dirty thieves. In the meantime, another bandit pinned my arms to my sides.

Spider strode forward. "Don't hurt them," he commanded in a stern, angry voice. "I said don't hurt them if you value your heads."

I struggled in the arms of my captor. He chuckled evilly in my ear as if he were enjoying it. "Maybe we can wrestle for pleasure sometime," he said.

I tried to flip him with one of the maneuvers Father had taught me, but I couldn't get the right leverage. So in desperation I kicked back with my heel and caught him right in the shin.

He let out an angry yowl and I found myself flying through the air, the wall looming before me. I tried to put out my hands, but it was too late. My head hit hard against the plaster, and then I was sliding down into the darkness, unconscious.

Chapter Sixteen

The kitchen was a shambles, the bowls and dishes broken and the rice half spilled out of the baskets. Someone had twisted a shirt so that it was like a rope and used it to bind Father's hands behind his back while a pair of trousers had been wound around his ankles. My hands and feet had been tied up too.

Spider had his back to me as he finished tying up Foxfire. "Now if you're as smart as I think you are, you won't wake up your father or sister until we're gone. I managed to keep my men under control this time, but I might not be able to the next time. Your father came within a millimeter of losing his life, and your sister could have been raped before they cut her throat."

Foxfire stared up at him accusingly. "Father believed in you and your Revolution."

Spider rose, dusting off his hands as if his own conscience were clear. "Your father remembers a younger and better Revolution, when there were more people like himself and your mother. But they only managed to get themselves killed off—and we're still no closer to saving the country."

But Foxfire wasn't about to let him off so easily. "And what do you believe in now?"

Spider took some rags and threw them across some broken jars to stop a pool of liquid from spreading. "I believe in my country and its people. And I'll do anything to make them strong again."

Suddenly a man gave a sharp, hurt cry; and then a woman began to scream, first in rage, then in fear.

"I can't allow them out of my sight for one moment." Spider gave a worried, exasperated sigh. I closed my own eyes quickly so he wouldn't know I was awake. His feet seemed to thud heavily as he ran off to try and stop his men. More voices were shouting now.

When I was sure he was gone, I opened my eyes and called to Father. "Wake up."

"Let him sleep," Foxfire scolded me in alarm. "He'll just get himself killed."

I remembered that look on Father's face. Was he angry enough to do something reckless if I woke him up? But what if I let him sleep through the raid? "It's going to be a nightmare for him one way or the other."

"But at least he'll be alive," Foxfire said.

I hadn't been able to make up my mind until Foxfire said that. I gave him a contemptuous look. "We're humans—not worms that crawl around on their bellies. Living isn't the important thing: It's how you live." And then I wriggled toward Father until I was right next to him. I butted him in the back with my head. "Father, wake up."

Father stirred. I butted him again. "Please wake up. The clan needs you." The cries outside had fused together into one terrible sound like a great, wounded beast howling in pain. It made my nerves feel all raw and jagged.

Father's eyes popped open, and he shook his head as if to clear it. "Are you all right?" he asked me.

"Yes, but the bandits are looting the other houses now." I tried to loosen the bonds around my wrists; but Spider and his friends had done too good a job.

When Father couldn't free himself either, he flipped onto his side so that his back was to me. "See if you can untie the knots with your teeth."

"You really can't mean to go out there." Foxfire watched in disbelief as I leaned forward to sink my teeth into the cloth of the knot. In the meantime, Father kicked and wriggled his legs, trying to loosen the bonds around his ankles.

"We can't let those dogs spoil everything." He spoke with some of his old confidence.

In sheer frustration, Foxfire thumped his heels against the floor. "Spoil what? What's the Work ever gotten us? Mother's dead, and you're crippled."

"Talk with more respect to me," Father said, scowling as if he were trying to frighten Foxfire into being quiet.

But Foxfire stayed defiant. "Then do something to earn my respect—like being sensible. Why don't you take your own advice for a change: You may have the heart of a warrior, but you don't have the legs of one anymore." Foxfire must have been saving that dark, poisonous thought all this time.

Father was silent for a while, as if he were hunting for a suitable answer and not having much success. And in the meantime I found that though the knot around Father's wrist was a large one, it had been tied so tightly that all my tugging and twisting couldn't worry it open.

During all this, Father had been trying to free his ankles with some more kicks; but suddenly he lay stunned. "They're setting fire to the village."

I sniffed the air, but it was a moment before the acrid smoke stung my nose. "This is taking too long," I said finally. "Maybe I can back in and untie you with my hands." I turned my back to him and then, looking over my shoulder to orient myself, I wormed over to him again.

If Foxfire hadn't been so desperate and upset, he might not have said what he did. "Do we all have to wind up with Mother before you'll be happy? Face facts. You've wasted all our lives on a lie."

Father didn't answer. He just lay in an angry, wounded silence.

I know Mother had asked me to watch out for my brother; but I don't think she had ever foreseen a night quite like this when he would question everything for which she and Father had fought. Even so, would Mother have put the Work before everything else? Or would she have figured it was more important to keep peace within our family? Right now the two most important things in her life seemed to be pulling in opposite directions.

But as idiotic as my brother was, he had good intentions. I suppose he was more worried about our safety than our reputations. So despite my own annoyance with him, I tried to protect Foxfire. I was afraid that Father might beat him once he got free. "Please remember that it's the bandits who are our real enemies. Not your son." My fingers tugged and pulled at the knot until I finally felt one of the ends begin to slip away from the other.

Father did not say anything for a long time while I went on working at his bonds. When he finally did speak, it was in a voice icy enough to freeze the flames in the village. "I have no son. No child of mine would call my life a lie."

"You can't hide from the truth," Foxfire argued. But he sounded terribly hurt.

Father refused to answer him. It was as if his son no longer existed. "Don't stand on principle," I said, trying to coax Father.

"Maybe that's all we have left now." Father kept his face toward the wall, as if he were trying to look through it toward the village.

"Maybe that's all you ever had." Panic had begun

to edge Foxfire's voice. "Maybe the Work was never anything more than a dream. And maybe it's time you woke up to the way people really are."

"Let me do the talking," I snapped at Foxfire. For a change, he listened to me. "Be kind to Foxfire," I said to Father. "I know you think he might be a fool and a coward; but he means well. Don't do anything hasty. You know you'll regret it later. Try and see things from Foxfire's viewpoint. Mother would have."

Father didn't say anything to me until the loop finally gave. Sitting upright immediately, he pulled his arms from behind his back. "I'll get to you as soon as I start my blood going again."

"And Foxfire?" I asked cautiously.

Father made a point of taking his time to rub the circulation back into his wrists. "I think the bandits are already gone." From outside, we could hear the urgent yells as the clan tried to form a human chain. Buckets of our precious water supply would have to be thrown onto the flames, or we might lose the whole village.

I looked over my shoulder at Father as he untied my wrists. "Maybe you'd better stay inside here then," I said. "They might blame you for what's happened."

"Then their minds have to be set straight on that

point. Spider and his men are not carrying on the Work." When Father had freed his ankles, he concentrated all his fury on flinging the bindings away.

"Father, I was only trying to be realistic." Foxfire now sounded as frightened and anxious as a small boy.

Father got to his feet uncertainly, almost falling at first; his feet must still have been numb from lack of blood. "Join me when you can, Cassia," he said to me as if there were no one else to talk to.

Foxfire said in a softer, more doubtful voice, "Father, don't shut me out like this. I was just trying to do what I thought was right."

But Father only heard the crackle of flames outside. A bright light spilled through the window and the doorway, catching each harsh line on his face. For a moment he seemed like some statue of a long-suffering warrior who can only see more years of trouble ahead of him and perhaps a cold, lonely grave.

When Father spoke, it seemed to be to the empty air. "I have fought for my dreams all my life. I intend to die fighting for them."

"Father?" Foxfire was almost sobbing now. "Don't you see? All your life you've chased after dreams and only been paid with shadows."

[173]

Father hesitated, but did not ask what Foxfire meant. "What are you talking about?" I asked as I bent forward to work on the bindings around my ankles.

Foxfire made his way over to me on his knees. "You know. The story about the rich man and the chef."

Mother had told us about a famous chef who used to go to rich people's houses to cook meals. He was so much in demand that rich people used to have to make appointments months in advance just to have him come and cook.

So this rich man had made an appointment for the most expensive banquet. He told the chef to spare no expense in purchasing the ingredients. But the night before the chef was supposed to come and cook the banquet, the rich man had a dream in which he sat in his huge palace at a large, round table. The chef himself served every dish personally. Each dish was better than the last. The fish and shrimp tasted as if they had come from the tables of the dragon king, and the quail and other fowl tasted as if they had been fed only with peaches from Heaven. The rich man never filled up but ate and ate, his tongue taking in new delights with every bite.

When the rich man woke up and found himself

in bed, he knew no mortal chef could ever serve a banquet to equal the one in his dreams. So he canceled his evening with the real chef.

Now the chef didn't lose any money because of it. He simply juggled the appointments in his books and found a rich man who was more then happy to pay him for the banquet planned by the other man. But the chef decided that this might set a bad precedent for his business. What if other rich people started dreaming of his banquets and canceling other appointments? So he sued the rich man for payment for the banquet that the chef had cooked during the dream.

They both had their day in court. The rich man explained his side of the case and the chef had his turn. Well, the magistrate thought and thought before he finally ordered the rich man to fill a vase full of gold coins. And then he told the chef to hold out his hands with his palms up. The chef did so with a smug smile. But then the magistrate ordered the rich man to move the vase in such a way that its shadow crossed the chef's open palms.

And then the magistrate announced, "For dreams, a person pays and is paid with shadows."

I frowned at Foxfire. "Mother used that story to show how the magistrates always favored the rich."

"But it means more than that." Foxfire turned around to me. "All their lives, Father and Mother have dreamed of the Revolution—and look at how they've been paid."

I started to free Foxfire. "And just what makes you think the golden mountain isn't just another shadow?"

Foxfire sat on his heels. "I just hurt both of you. Maybe we'd all be better off if I went to the golden mountain. One way or another, some of your problems would be solved."

Slowly, like some statue learning to walk, Father limped toward the door, but he paused on the threshold. "Maybe you should."

"Father," I said sharply. "You don't mean that."

He hesitated on the threshold as if he were weakening. But the light of the fire was full in his face, and the shouting had increased. That seemed to harden his resolve. With a little shake of his head, he refused to take back his words. Then it was too late as he stepped outside.

"He'll come around." Whether I was getting better with practice or Spider had tied Foxfire's hands more loosely than ours, I didn't have any trouble untying the knot. "Just give him time."

"You don't think that I'm a fool and a coward too,

do you, Cassia?" Foxfire's eyes searched my face for some kind of denial.

I knew what he wanted to hear. And under normal circumstances I might have tried to make him feel better. But at that moment my mind was taken up more with Father. I could hear him shouting to someone to bring him more water. At least for the moment, everyone was too busy putting out the fire to blame anyone. I wanted to be out there before they did.

I got to my feet carefully. "No," I said, "but sometimes you give a good imitation of both." And then, Heaven have mercy on me, I hobbled outside, leaving my little brother to finish freeing himself.

Chapter Seventeen

It was nearly dawn by the time we had put out the fires. When we were finished, we simply stared at the blackened timbers. Though there were no more flames, smoke still rose from the coals and ashes.

"I can't believe the Work has come to this." Father wiped a hand across his smudged forehead, blackening the skin even more. Bad leg and all, he had still been battling the blaze at the very front of the line.

Now that the danger was over, the Golden Cat appeared near the ruins so he could collar Uncle Windy. "A house lost and two more damaged. This is all Spider's fault." Though his voice was hoarse from bellowing orders from the rear of the bucket brigade, his clothes had stayed immaculately clean.

Uncle Windy began to squeal like a trapped rat. "No, no. He hasn't been my son for a long time now. But even if he was, it's all the Gallant's fault. He's the one who ruined Spider." And he jabbed his index finger frantically at Father.

One by one, people began to turn toward us, their faces sullen and bitter. Father spread out his hands. "Those bandits weren't my friends."

A woman yelled back, "They were collecting for the Revolution, weren't they?"

Others of the clan began to gather around, eager to have a target for their rage. When I saw someone pick up a stone, I set my back protectively against Father's and looked for Foxfire.

Father raised his voice so that more people could hear him. "You've only got yourselves to blame for this, you know. If you'd helped us with the Work, Spider wouldn't have had to turn to the bandits."

As the people began to murmur angrily to one another, Uncle Blacky elbowed his way to the front and pivoted, raising his hands. "Now wait. The bandits would have come here anyway." He had to duck as a stone flew over his head. It missed us by only a few centimeters.

"There." Father pointed toward the crowd. "You've just seen an idiot's answer to the truth."

I was frightened when I saw other members of the clan stooping to pick up bits of rubble to throw. Uncle Blacky ran around trying to reason with them; but he might as well have been a fly for all the attention they paid him.

"Foxfire," I called out desperately to the mob. "We need you." And when there wasn't any answering call, I tried again. "Foxfire. Hurry." When there still wasn't any response, I turned to Father. "Do you think something's happened to Foxfire?"

Father's voice was hard and unrelenting. "Foxfire who?"

I turned around and gripped his sleeve. "Your son."

He stared down at me. "I have no son."

The others of the clan stood there puzzled. "What do you mean?" the Golden Cat demanded.

Father set his face into a solemn mask. "I've disowned my boy."

The Golden Cat wrinkled his forehead in disbelief. "But he's your only son."

Father drew himself up as bravely as he could. "It's a small loss."

"But who's going to send you food and money

when you pass on?" The Golden Cat wanted to know.

Most people worried about the time after they had died but before they were born again. It was important to them that their spirits receive things to use in the land of the dead. (You didn't actually send money or food, but bought special paper cutouts and burned those).

"I'll see that Father has everything he needs," I volunteered. "He won't have to beg in the land of the dead."

"You'll be married soon, girl." The Golden Cat dismissed me with a stern wave of his hand. "And then you'll owe your duty to your husband's parents."

"Maybe I won't get married." I tossed my head back defiantly.

"Don't talk like a fool," Father snapped at me.

"Your children are enough of a penance to have to bear." The Golden Cat nodded to me.

I checked my angry retort. This was no time to work up the mob with another argument. People were now less angry and more curious. It was bad enough to disown a son as Uncle Windy had done; but at least he had Sticks to see that he was provided for in the afterlife. Losing an only son was an even more drastic punishment for my father than being stoned. Bruises and broken bones from stones would heal in time. But disowning Foxfire meant a life of poverty in the afterlife. Folk began throwing away the debris they had picked up before.

I decided to risk trying to leave. "Help me look for Foxfire."

"I told you." Father shook his head with a savage jerk. "I have no child by that name."

I was beginning to feel bad about what I had said to my brother. He was sensitive in his own way; and no matter how stupid he had been when we were children, Mother had never gotten mad at him.

"I have a brother, though," I insisted. "And I'm going to find him." I took a step toward the crowd. "Excuse me," I said to them, and people elbowed one another to get out of my way.

"Wait," Father growled. "I'll help you search for that creature."

"Where do you want me to look?" the good-hearted Uncle Blacky asked.

"You've your own family to take care of, friend." Patting Uncle Blacky on the shoulder, Father started down the lane.

Foxfire wasn't in our house nor in any of the houses

on the lane. In fact, he didn't seem to be in the village at all. I thought he might be sulking down in the fields, but he wasn't there either. And when I went to the cemetery along the ridgetop, we found only Aster. She was standing among the pines, anxiously surveying the moonlit valley below.

"Have you seen Tiny?" she asked. "I've looked everywhere for him."

I knelt beside my mother's grave, brushing the dirt from her stone marker. It was time that I faced the last unpleasant possibility. "No, have you seen my brother?"

"They were together just a few hours ago." Aster plucked some of the needles from the branch of a pine tree.

I rested my hand on the grave marker. Why, oh, why hadn't I stayed with him just a little longer and talked to him? I reminded myself that I had been worried about Father. After all, I couldn't be in two places at once. But that didn't work. There had still been time to ease Foxfire's hurts so he wouldn't keep thinking of running away. "They wouldn't have been talking about the golden mountain, would they?"

Aster crushed the pine needles between her palms and sniffed the scent. "You know your brother. That's all that's on his mind." Aster suddenly opened her hands. "Oh, no. You don't think they ran off together to the golden mountain?"

"The boy's all talk and no action," Father said, but even he didn't sound as sure anymore.

"They probably just went off to town to earn a little money." But I couldn't look at either of them, concentrating instead on cleaning the marker in my nervousness. Right at that moment I felt even worse than when we had sold the window. I had promised my mother to take care of my little brother, but I'd only managed to help drive him away. It was as if I had killed that small part of Mother that had stayed inside me. And I'd failed to keep my own promise to myself that my little brother and I were never going to be apart.

More than ever, I wished my mother were alive now so I could just rest my head in her lap and let her sort out the tangled mess I had helped make.

Tiny came to our house that evening. He had a large bruise under one eye that made me suspect that he had already seen Aster. In his hands were several strings of cash. "Foxfire sent these to you." He fingered the money as if he were slightly embarrassed. "He also said you probably wouldn't mind giving me a little."

I stared at the strings of cash. "How did he get these?"

"They advance you money when you go overseas." Tiny thrust the strings out toward me, but I didn't want to touch them. I felt like the coins had been coated in poor Foxfire's blood.

"Overseas?" Father leaned against a wall for support. "I didn't think he had that kind of courage. He never showed it before."

"Maybe he never had anything he thought was worth fighting for." I gazed eastward. There was so much we didn't know about the trip. How large was the ocean he would have to cross? What was the demon land really like? And what would my little brother do without me to protect him? I felt myself grieving for him as if he were already dead.

"Maybe it's not too late to catch him." Father shoved himself away from the wall.

"No, I saw him off on the riverboat that was going to take him to the seaport." Tiny added with boyish enthusiasm, "They say there's a huge ship waiting to take him overseas."

Suddenly a new and more frightening thought came to me as I remembered what the coolies had said. I swung around toward Tiny again. "And just how did he buy his passage overseas? We don't own our fields or our house."

Tiny jingled the strings apologetically. "I put myself up as his bond."

"Oh, my stars." My grief turned to shame and I pressed my palms over my reddening cheeks. I looked over at Father and saw that his legs had given out completely, and he plopped down onto the floor.

"Don't worry. He'll pay it off soon." The loyal Tiny tried to defend his friend. It never occurred to that bighearted man that his friend might not survive.

Father and I exchanged glances and it seemed as we were sharing the same thoughts. As sure as the sun rose in the east, something bad was bound to happen to my impractical, absentminded brother. And poor Tiny would be doomed to a life of slavery. In my own imagination, I could see poor Tiny being carted off to be sold. It wasn't a question of "if" but of "when."

If Foxfire had been there at the moment, I would have kicked him across the room. How could he have placed Tiny in such a terrible predicament? Then I reminded myself that it was my fault. After all, I had been the one to run off after Father instead of letting him get the talk out of his system. I sighed, knowing that I would have to shoulder the responsibility for all of this.

Tiny stretched out his arms from his sides. He was puzzled by all the fuss we were making. "Really, it's Foxfire who's taking all the risks."

"But you're the one who will suffer the most if something goes wrong. Death is far easier than slavery." Father struggled back to his feet. "I can't let that happen to you."

"What are you going to do?" I asked, but I already suspected what was on Father's mind—because I had the same idea.

"Go into town in the morning. If I can't get the boy back, I'll put myself up as his bond instead of Tiny." Father took the strings of cash from Tiny. "You're a good friend—better than he deserves."

"But I was glad to help," Tiny protested.

"This is something his . . . his family has to do." Father sounded almost sorry that he had to use that word to refer to the bond between himself and Fox-fire.

"I'll go too," I offered. Father opened his mouth to argue, but I stilled him with a look. "I don't even like to think about my life here without you and him."

Father rubbed his bad leg. "Well, the merchants might not take a crippled, middle-aged man in place of a muscular young one like Tiny. But perhaps they'll be willing to accept the exchange if you're thrown into the deal as well."

When we went to town, we wound up talking to the same clerk who had bought our furniture. As we started to argue with him, he got this funny look on his face—as if we were two shaggy, half-starved beasts who had just escaped from their cage. Motioning several of the other clerks over in case we got violent, he told us it was impossible to bring Foxfire back because the boat taking him to the seaport would already have sailed. I wasn't sure of that, but I would have hated to use up so much of our cash to go to the seaport only to find him gone.

The clerk didn't even want to let us exchange ourselves for Tiny; but he gave in when we looked ready to tear the store apart.

Both Father and I paused outside the store when the paperwork was finished. Though neither of us said it, we both knew that it was only a matter of time before the clerk came to claim us. Suddenly Father lifted the bag that held the strings of cash. "What should we do with this?"

I wrapped my arms around myself. "We should give half of it to Tiny."

"I assumed we were going to do that." Father clinked the bag against his leg. "I was asking you what we ought to do with our half." He shifted his feet uncomfortably. "It . . . seems almost like blood money now."

I patted his arm. "You couldn't know he'd run overseas. I thought he'd just sulk in the house for a while."

Father watched the people stream by the storefront. "I never had any trouble understanding you, Cassia. You're a fighter like me. I knew I could always count on you. But Foxfire was always so different. Whenever I tried to talk to him about the Work or teach him the martial arts, I always had this feeling that he retreated into this little fortress inside himself. And he would mock me in secret."

It was a moment that required all of Mother's wisdom and skill, but I had neither. All I could come up with was a lame statement. "He was always afraid that he was disappointing you."

Father glanced sideways at me. "But he said all those things about the Work, too."

I shrugged guiltily, remembering all the harsh

things that were said that night. I wished I had been able to look at things more objectively then. "He was just feeling frustrated by what Spider had done. The Work was a handy target."

I'll never forget that agonized look on Father's face—like a warrior who's been disarmed and stands waiting for a deathblow. "Target? You make the Work sound like it's just a piece of junk."

"You know I believe in the Work," I said. "I was just trying to help you see Foxfire's viewpoint. As you said, the Work is the important thing. It's more important than any of us."

Father wrapped his arms around himself like a beggar trying to cover himself in a tattered cloak. "I may not have my leg," he said quietly. "I may not have my sworn brothers anymore." He lifted his head. "But that doesn't mean the Work itself is wrong. Its ideals are still the good and true ones: peace and freedom and prosperity for all."

Now that the Brotherhood had turned away from its high principles, Father's faith and pride were all that he had left. So I chose my words with care. "Foxfire would have come around once he had time to think."

"You see? I just don't know how to be his father." He slapped his hand against his leg. "I used to hope that something magical would happen and the knowledge would come as a grace from Heaven. But it never did." He sighed. "And now it's too late."

Father had always seemed so strong and sure about things in the past that his confession frightened me now. I gave a shiver. "It's too late for us all, I guess."

Father forced himself to smile as he held the bag up again. "Well, condemned prisoners should have at least one good meal before they march off into slavery."

Perhaps I should have put on a long face and gone moping back to the valley, but instead I felt a false sense of elation. It was one of only a dozen times that I'd been away from Three Willows, so the town was always exciting to me. The prospect of a real meal cooked by someone else made me feel almost regal. I told myself that our troubles weren't going to get any better whether I worried about them or not. I told myself that we deserved at least a few moments of enjoyment. I would have plenty of time to fret tomorrow. "Yes," I said, taking Father's hand, "let's have supper."

With the rest of our money we bought rice and vegetables as well as seed for that winter's vegetable crops. But when we returned to the village, Tiny didn't want to take his half of the money.

"I just wanted one string. After all, I'm not the one who's making the voyage," he said.

"Take them," Father insisted. And though Tiny was a head taller and was a good deal heavier and better muscled, Father looked ready to pound some sense into Tiny's head.

"If you won't take them for your sake, take it for Aster's," I urged.

"Are you sure you want to do this?" Tiny stared at the money unhappily.

"We're positive." Father grabbed Tiny's hands and forced the money into them.

"Foxfire never planned on this much." Tiny scratched his head uneasily.

"He doesn't have much say in the matter now," Father snapped.

Chapter Eighteen

The first month was hard. It was a surprise to learn how much I missed my little brother. I hadn't noticed how long the days could be until I no longer had Foxfire's bright chatter to distract me when I worked in the fields. And there was no one to help me at night with the dozens of little chores that had to be done at the house. But most of all there was no one who had quite his imagination. Aster could make me laugh; but she didn't have Foxfire's whimsical streak. His absence left almost as big a gap in my life as the selling of the lattice left in our wall. I had never realized how much like Mother he was.

I began to think about all the times he had exasperated me, and much to my shame, I began to see how trivial they had been. My days seemed dull and empty now that Foxfire was no longer there to color them with bits of his whimsy. But of course, there was no way to tell him that now.

In my own mind my little brother was as good as dead. At night, my mind pictured all the horrible things that the demons might be doing to him: dumping him in boiling cauldrons of oil or in pits of scorpions and any other number of tortures like the other demons do to the dead. All he had to remember of me were harsh words.

Even Father seemed to regret some of the things he had said to Foxfire. In the mornings when we exercised together, Father corrected me with a gentleness he had never shown before. Finally one day he paused in adjusing the position of my arms. "Do you think Foxfire will remember anything I taught him?"

I tried an experimental turn. "I hope so. It might keep him alive."

Father stepped back with a nod. "Maybe I should have taught him simpler things."

I whipped my arms through the air and then gave a high kick. "He would have gotten those things wrong too. He had it in his head that he just couldn't do it."

The frustration made Father's tongue stumble. "Maybe I expected too much of him. But it's . . . it's just that I wanted him to be the next gallant in the village."

I stopped. "I wish we could have seen him for what he really was: a gentle dreamer." It seemed natural to think of Foxfire in the past tense now.

When the second and then the third month passed and we still didn't hear from the clerk, the clan began to treat us like two animals marked for the slaughter. I'd already heard that several couples had asked if they could rent our house when we were gone. (Our house, like our fields, belonged to the Golden Cat.)

But the fourth month was the hardest as our precious food stores dwindled steadily even though I began to make rice gruels. It was a dreary enough New Year. And to add to our miseries, the winter rains did not come with their usual force, so the winter vegetables came up stunted and a sickly yellow. As Father and I sometimes joked to one another, we might actually cheat the clerk if he waited much longer to come.

The poorer members of the clan seemed to resign

themselves to the fact that they were going to die. Their stomachs began taking on the odd, bloated look of the starved. People became so weak from hunger that the slightest illness killed them before they could starve to death. The clan treasury even ran out of money to clothe folk in their old age—a polite phrase for burying people in coffins. The poorer families had to dig holes and stick their loved ones into the ground as if they were merely dead pigs.

Still, we all tried to go through the motions of living. Father continued leading the militia, and I went on trying to tend our fields.

Two stars began to appear at night just above the horizon. They were the tips of the horns of the constellation known as the dragon; and people used to know it was time to begin the spring planting when they saw the bright, sharp tips of its horns ready to impale the moon.

And even though the dry, parched earth was as hard as stone, we did our best to break it with hoes to prepare it for the first rice crop. But by the end of one afternoon, I barely had the strength to stump up the zig-zagging path that led to the village.

A fine dust now covered the statue of the Earth Lord in his little shrine, and a breeze stirred the small mound of ashes in front of him—all that was left of the burned incense sticks. A tentacle of ashes trailed outward, caught under the belly of the breeze, and strips of paper flapped on a stick thrust into the ground. Once a bright red, the strips had been quickly faded by the sun to a sickly pinkish color, but I could still make out the words written in the scholarly hand of Uncle Blacky. I did not know the words, but I had been told that they were a petition to the Earth Lord and the other gods and dragons who might be responsible for the drought—reminding them that Heaven let them keep their offices by competence, not by right.

A lot of good the prayers and incense had done.

Even worse, though, was the silence in Three Willows. Usually there were children tumbling in and out of the houses, or a mother singing a lullaby, or someone working to a rhythmic chánt: but no one had the energy anymore. The children were either too tired or too hungry to play. The only sound was a lid landing occasionally on a wok—but even this sound was rarer and rarer as food became scarce.

The worst thing about the drought was the feeling of helplessness: that no matter how long we worked in the fields and how hard we prayed, the plants continued to wither and die—and so would we, one by one.

The once warm, friendly walls of our courtyard—walls that had sheltered our family for hundreds of years—suddenly seemed like the walls of a trap.

I looked down at the small bundle of weeds I had gathered. We were reduced to weed soup once again. I don't know what had made me think I could take Mother's place. Not only was the Work in a shambles, but I'd helped break up our family. I couldn't even put a decent meal on the table—assuming that we had any furniture. I was feeling so dry and empty inside that I couldn't cry—and that only added to my frustration.

Suddenly I heard feet thudding down the lane. It was an odd sound when people barely had the vitality to shuffle nowadays. The footsteps came right to our house, and then Aster was pounding at the gates. "Cassia, the clerk's in the valley and he's asking for you or your father."

So the day had finally come when we received the terrible news. A wordless scream tried to work its way up my throat like some determined little mole. But I told myself that I couldn't let myself fall apart—not now.

The clerk had probably come to claim us, and if that was true, there was a sacrifice that I could make for Father and the Work. Perhaps the clerk would settle for just me. If so, Father could continue to lead the militia against the Phoenixes—and perhaps even purify the Work somehow. I felt sure it was the kind of thing Mother would have done if she had been alive. And in a way I felt it was a fit punishment, since I'd failed to keep my vows to both Mother and myself to protect Foxfire.

Straightening my blouse, I opened the gates to find Aster panting for breath from her long run. "Please bring the clerk up."

"What?" Aster blinked her eyes in surprise.

"And don't send anyone to bring Father back from his patrol," I instructed her. "Wait until we're gone."

"But he would want to be here at least." Aster massaged her forehead with her fingertips.

"My father would never make a good slave." I tried to smile.

"Neither will you." Aster gave me a quick hug as she finally understood. "But I'll do what you want."

The other women of the lane had gathered. Some looked as if they pitied me. But there were a few who could not hide their satisfaction. It was as if they had known that Foxfire and I were doomed from the very beginning.

I shut the gates again. It's strange how vanity can take over even at a time like that. I wanted to clean up before I was taken away. I had nothing to pack, since we had sold even our spare clothing. But at least I could wash up.

As I went to get the water, I remembered all the fine things my brother had imagined about the golden mountain. Now his bones were probably lying somewhere upon a mountainside bleaching in the sun.

I was just finishing up when I heard the impatient knocking. My hands and feet felt numb, as if I were already dying bit by bit. But I managed to roll my sleeves and pants back down, and then I forced myself to walk across the courtyard. The air felt cool on the water beading my face.

I swung the left gate open to find our old friend, the clerk, was there to greet me. Behind him stood two smaller men, and in back of them were Aster and quite a few of the clan.

Well, I could show them how a serpent's child met her fate. "Can I help you?" I asked calmly enough.

But the clerk ignored me as if he had more important things on his mind. "I took out my master's commission already." One of his men shoved a package roughly into my arms. I was so startled by its heaviness that I dropped it; and I was even more surprised when it landed with a jingling sound.

"What's in that?" I stepped back, rubbing my fingers slowly against the sides of my blouse.

The clerk ignored me, speaking in a bored way as if he had already given the speech a number of times. "After this, we can arrange an account for you. We advise doing that since it's safer than transporting money into the hills."

I picked up the package again, cradling it in my arms. "An account? Whatever for?"

The clerk frowned as if I were unusually dense. "Why, for the remittances, of course."

I stared down, flustered. "These aren't my brother's remains?"

The clerk rolled his eyes Heavenward as if asking for strength and then looked back at me. "It's money. Your brother exchanged his gold for a letter of credit, which was then sent over here and converted into cash—for a slight fee."

I was so stunned that it took me a moment to find my voice. "You mean there really is gold on the mountain?"

"Obviously," the clerk snapped.

"But this package is so heavy, it can't all be cash," I protested.

"I can assure you that it is. Twenty strings, in fact." With an impatient nod of his head, he turned around and, followed by his men, started up the lane once again.

Aster was at my side in an instant. "Aren't you going to open it up? Better let me help you." She reached out her hands to take the package from me, but I clung to it.

"I've never seen twenty strings of cash all in the same place, have you?" I half expected the package to disappear at any moment—like the demon treasures in some of the stories.

"I've never *heard* of so much money in my life," Aster bubbled enthusiastically. "It's like having your own hoard of demon gold."

Tiny managed to shove his way through the crowd that now filled the entire lane. "You could have meat every day," he said gleefully, "just like the rich folk do." Normally we had meat only at New Year's—and in the last few years we hadn't even been able to afford that much.

"She *is* rich," Aster corrected her husband. "Her brother's sitting on top of the golden mountain." She patted me on the arm. "You've had the last laugh on us all."

"And Foxfire's alive," I laughed to Tiny and Aster. Already I could feel the tears beginning to roll down my cheeks. "He made it overseas."

"Well," Uncle Windy announced pompously to the crowd, "I always knew Foxfire was cleverer than people gave him credit for."

I was going to tell him that he had hidden it very well, but I held my peace. After all, I hadn't behaved any better. Nor had Father. Not even Mother had anticipated this moment. How had we all managed to miss that special something in Foxfire? His courage to fight for *his* dream if not for Father's.

Despite all the ridicule and doubting, he'd held to his dream and found it. And more than that. I glanced around at the clan. Many of them were so gaunt with hunger that the flesh was stretched tightly over their skulls. An outsider would probably have said they looked like zombies who had escaped from their graves; and yet their faces were lit up with hope. And it was my brother—the one whom I had called a fool—who had given them a new grip on life by going off and finding a real mountain of gold.

A cheer suddenly went up at the back of the crowd

and heads began to move and bob like so many leaves on a windy stream. "Make way, make way," I could hear Cricket shouting with immense self-importance. "Let him through." The little boy suddenly appeared, pushing and shoving at everyone else.

Puzzled, Father followed him, his spear resting against his right shoulder. "Cassia, what's going on?"

Trembling, I held up the package. "Foxfire's alive and he sent us this."

Father straightened up. "You mean he actually survived the trip?"

"And more than that." I rested the package on one hip. "The clerk says he sent us twenty strings of cash."

Father looked almost as shocked as I had been. "That I have to see." When he saw all the eager, curious faces surrounding him, he motioned me inside the house. "But in private."

He ignored the protests as we marched inside the courtyard; he had to do a little shoving to close the gates, and even then there were complaints that he had banged them shut against a few noses. When we entered the house, I dumped the package in the middle of the room.

"You must have heard it wrong. That can't all be money." Father set his spear in its usual corner.

"Well," I felt obligated to point out, "considering that you disowned him, it would be big of Foxfire to send us even one string."

"Maybe." Father rolled up his sleeves and circled the package as if he were puzzled.

"Please, Father. I can't wait any longer." I knelt beside the package.

"It's just that I expect it to vanish in a puff of smoke." Father squatted on the floor and paper and twine went flying. And there, in the center of the floor, was string after string of cash—each string with a thousand cash.

I picked up one of them and let it drop with a heavy clashing sound back upon the floor. "There are kilograms of cash here."

Father rested his chin against his chest guiltily. "It's a gift worthy of a prince."

It should have been a good, warm moment for the both of us, but Father looked as if Foxfire's generosity only made him feel ashamed.

"Loving takes different forms," I said, trying to comfort him.

Father reached his fingers out to poke the money cautiously. "I just hope there's enough here to please everyone."

I dragged one string of cash back and forth over

the floor. "You mean 'contributions' to the bandits? We've got to keep them away even if the Work hasn't been purified."

Father placed his hands on his knees and rocked to and fro. "And some help to the clan. And I've a few of the militia who could use a meal. . . ." His voice trailed off, but I knew there would be plenty of people who would be asking for a share.

To my dismay, I began to realize just how quickly this pile of cash would dwindle down. And then I shook off my mood. Who cared about the money? The important thing was that Foxfire was alive.

"Well, at least Foxfire's seen to it that we won't starve." As I picked up the wrapping paper to fold and save, an envelope plopped onto the floor. I blinked my eyes, but it didn't go away so I held it up. "I . . . I think Foxfire might have dictated a letter to someone."

Father simply gaped at the letter for a moment. "It's one thing for a scholar to write his own thoughts down; but it's another thing for common folk like us."

Cautiously I opened the envelope and took out the thick sheaf of pages. "It looks like a small book." I put my hands over the pages as if I might be able to understand them by touch alone. "Who will read it to us?" I asked in disappointment.

"I think I saw Uncle Blacky out there. I don't think he'd mind." Father got to his feet hurriedly, almost as eager to hear the letter as I was. I was so glad that, for the moment, he seemed to have forgotten that he had disowned his son. I guess Father did care for Foxfire in some deep, inner part of his heart.

Chapter Nineteen

When Uncle Blacky came into the house, he stared at the strings of cash just as we had.

Father held up a wine kettle. "Cassia, get some cups for us, will you? Our friends at the wine shop sent this." Father smiled ironically since "our friends" at the shop would not have given us credit as of just an hour ago. He glanced at the money, drawing his eyebrows together in a sad, puzzled way. "It's strange that a lifetime of effort has brought less respect than Foxfire's pile of money."

I think it grated Father's pride to realize how quickly and easily Foxfire had raised the status of our family. All his and Mother's sacrifices for the Work had not earned any respect for us. So as I got down some teacups, I hunted for something to ease the sting. "People would have come around anyway, but money just speeded up the process."

When I had poured the warm wine into the cups, Uncle Blacky tore his eyes away from the pile of money. Taking his cup, he raised it in a toast to Father. "As the saying goes, only the finest oyster produces the best pearl. Look at you. You can laugh at the famine now. And what adventures your son must have had."

Father shifted uncomfortably. Even now, in his relief that Foxfire was alive, and despite Foxfire's magnificent gift, Father didn't like going back on something he'd said about my brother. It was a matter of pride. "There's some fool over there who might think he's my son." Father picked up the envelope. "And he seems to have dictated a letter to some scholar over there. But we're such ignorant folk, we can't read it."

I was sure that Father was as anxious to hear the letter as I was, but it wouldn't have been polite to have thrust the envelope into Uncle Blacky's hands and demand that he read it to us. One didn't treat a man of learning as if he were some tailor.

"Well, why don't I read it?" Uncle Blacky offered.

"We could hardly think of asking you to use your great learning for such purposes," Father said, using his most formal manners. They argued back and forth for the sake of politeness until Uncle Blacky almost tore the envelope from Father's hands. When he had it, he frowned critically. "Oh dear. Look at those fat, stiff strokes. It's almost a schoolboy's scrawl."

"But you can read it?" Father asked.

Uncle Blacky opened the envelope carefully and took out the many thin sheets of paper. "Yes, but you'll have to bear with me. It might take me a while to puzzle my way through certain parts." He rattled the sheets of paper and cleared his throat before he began to read:

"I am writing to you through the kindness of my friend Smiley. Since I have been disowned as your son, I suppose that makes me a ghost—at least on paper. Even so, I must insist on speaking to you from 'beyond the grave.'

"I made it overseas, and if I live to be a hundred years old, I do not think I could describe half the wonders of this strange land. The demons' city of San Francisco is the oddest place. Because no one had time to build proper houses, they live in hundreds of ships that are rotting at the piers because all the sailors have left to search for gold. And beyond the ships, men and demons live in tents, and the dirty gray sides flap and boom in the wind—as if they were fat pigeons preening themselves on the barren hills.

"There are a few buildings of mud and some more of wood. The planks are so new that they gleam a golden white—as if they had been sliced from the mellowing bones of giants. I almost think a good strong wind could carry the entire city away.

"A few of our merchants have settled in the demon city. These clerks and storekeepers try to act as if the demon city does not exist at all. They stay in their own section and they dress exactly as they would at home. They even take great pains to shave the crowns of their heads each morning and wash their hair carefully before they braid it. Their meals and most of their daily routine are exactly as they would be at home.

"But every night I was reminded that this little patch of home was only an illusion. Through the canvas sides of the tents, I could see the silhouettes of demons and demonesses until the tent sides seemed like the screens of that puppet master who once visited Three Willows. Only these are strange shadow puppets chirping and yowling and growling in the demons' bird-and-beast talk.

[211]

"Now and then outlandish men roar into the tents. They call themselves 'guests' of the golden mountain—I think as an ironic joke; for their lives are far from easy with so many demons as their hosts. These guests dress partly in the demonic fashion and their talk is studded with bird-and-beast sounds that they have learned from their hosts. And these guests scatter gold dust like lords; and the clerks and storekeepers flutter around them eager to please.

"It didn't take me long to be hired. My employer is a Fragrant Mountain man who has guested among the demons from the very early days of the search for gold. He is usually fair in his dealings. He told me that I will have to pay for my own food, mainly rice and dried fish and vegetables, which must be bought from the merchants in the city. It is a common practice, so I cannot complain.

"Even so, I am not discouraged. This is not the place for such thoughts. Here a person can dream, a person can plan; and there are no scholars and no clan elders to tell you what to do. And the rich merchants are far away in the city. My employer has no one to order him about except his own whims."

"That's hard to imagine." Father scratched his cheek.

Uncle Blacky fanned himself thoughtfully with a

page of the letter. "Harder even than palaces carved from whole mountains of jade."

Father pointed at the other pages. "But what else does he have to say?"

Uncle Blacky continued:

"There is a tremendous force in this land that breeds a taste for solitude. Everywhere, a person finds machines rather than people. When I left the city with my new employer, we traveled in a big, funny riverboat—like a square floating house with two stories and a big paddle wheel in the stern. The boat chugged along, complete and self-contained, needing no sails to catch the wind or men to pull it along, but only its own self. Sitting on the deck, I could feel the power throb through its decks; and its smokestacks scattered a fine black soot with equal contempt over human and demon alike.

"This land is so big and wild. We passed through a string of bays up a river into a vast valley of rich virgin meadowlands—such lands as our own valley at home might have been when the first Young founded Three Willows. You can feel the life nearly bursting through the soil. The sheer waste of it. The weeds alone would have provided Three Willows with fuel and mulch for years.

"But it is not in these pretty meadowlands that

one finds the true virtue of the demon wilderness. It begins in the hills, where only a single tree may grow in some hollow; for it seems that only grasses and weeds will grow there. They are already a golden, tawny color like a fur I saw once. It is as if the grass had been stretched over supple muscle. When the wind passes over the hillsides, it is as if an invisible gigantic hand were stroking the shoulders of the land to try to soothe it. Even the rolling outline of the hills has a raw, naked, muscular look.

"At that point we had to get off the boat and join the stream of men and demons flowing deeper into the wilderness. Away from the river, even the hills seemed to fall apart, the soil giving way to great slabs of rock that reared upward from the withered grass like watchmen. And the rocks gave way in turn to sheer-sided mountains upon which only odd, cone-shaped trees grew, as if even the plant life must take on the shape of the mountains.

"It was here that I first began to notice large stretches of land that had been laid waste. It was as if some giant beast had bitten into the hillsides and spat out huge, dirty mounts of slag. It was only when we reached the gold fields that I understood why. There may have been a golden mountain here once, but all its bits and pieces are scattered around the other mountains now."

Father shook his head, puzzled. "How can you live in a place without respecting the harmonies of nature?"

"Well, it's the demons' land," Uncle Blacky said, and went on:

"You would not believe how cold this land can get compared to home. There is even snow on the ground. Cool and dazzling white, it makes grunting noises when I walk on it. I have had to borrow money from my employer to get a solid coat and thick boots made by the demons. We all waddle around like pregnant ducks.

"Our day begins at sunrise, when we get up to dig shovelfuls of dirt and put into a big trough. Then we use a water pump just like at home to bring water from a nearby stream into the trough, and the water sweeps the dirt away. The gold, being heavier than the dirt, falls to the bottom of the trough and gathers along cleats on the bottom. After we collect the gold dust, we dry it at night by a fire inside the cabin.

"So you see, we men and demons, as small as we may be, are gradually wearing down the very heart of this wilderness. You needn't worry about me. I'm well settled in. The work is hard, but the air here is as heady as wine: and the talk is even headier. It's too bad that Cassia wasn't born a boy. She would have made a far better son for you than I ever will. I could never accept the Work anymore."

I had been watching Father's face; and up to that point he had been smiling in a warm, interested way. So I began to think that I might be able to make Father back down from his proud stand and acknowledge Foxfire as his son again.

But when Uncle Blacky read that last sentence, Father stiffened suddenly as if someone had lashed him across an old wound. He regarded the pile of cash suspiciously now. "What's he really trying to do with that money? Show how superior his way is?"

"Of course not," I said, but I almost wished that Foxfire hadn't written the letter now—or at least just stuck to the facts.

"Well, you heard him. He wouldn't apologize." Father waved a hand at the letter. "And he's as good as said that the Work means nothing. He'd rather fill his head with exotic kinds of nonsense."

I remembered what Father had said in town: that all he had now was his faith in the Work. "Let Uncle Blacky finish," I said desperately. "Maybe there's something else in the letter that explains what he means."

Uncle Blacky began to read hastily before Father could say anything else:

"And, in fact, I am more convinced than ever that this land will shape our future from now on. We are a new community with much to learn and discuss. I plunge into the icy cold waters of the mountain streams each morning to wake myself up. And at night I dive into a river of new, exciting ideas."

"There, you see. He talks about 'new, exciting ideas' as if the Work were just an antique," Father grumbled.

"There's just a little bit more," Uncle Blacky said diplomatically.

"I know there were hard words between us when we parted; but I won't tell you that I'm sorry. As you yourself said on another occasion, I should never apologize when I think I've done the right thing. I realize the money cannot ease all your hurts. If I could give you the Empire, I would; but all I can do is present you with your own little kingdom to rule as you please. It will take some four years to work off my debts, but I can stay and earn money for as long as you like. So go ahead and buy yourself a scholarly title and get one of those guns you have always wanted and whatever else you need to keep the justice and peace in your own little patch of dirt—if in no other place.

"Well, it's late now and I have to end my letter here, as my friend's eyes and hand are getting tired."

Uncle Blacky peered more closely at the last page. "There's a second handwriting that's even worse than the first." He looked up in surprise. "I think Foxfire's tried to sign his own name." He lowered his eyes again. "It says, 'The Ghost of Increase of Prosperity.'" Increase of Prosperity was Foxfire's formal name.

And when I heard that, I knew that my little brother was still hurting over his last night in the village. I wanted to reach out and hug Foxfire and tell him that things would be all right. It had always worked when we were small, but I had to remind myself that we were no longer children. Maybe if Father and I had seen he was almost a man, we would have thought more about the things we'd said to him. It made me ache inside to think that there was nothing I could do over that long distance that now separated Foxfire from us.

Uncle Blacky laid the last page down. "There, you see. Those 'new ideas' were probably the plans he was making for you. But you could really do most anything you wanted. Once the bankers hear you have a son who's a 'guest' of the golden mountain, they'll be swarming all over here trying to lend you money. I suppose you're going to buy some fields at least."

Father rubbed his chin thoughtfully, as if he disliked having to go along with any of Foxfire's suggestions. I was afraid that he might be stubborn enough to refuse. But eventually he admitted, "Well, I suppose a few fields would be nice."

I breathed a sigh of relief, and when he glanced at me, I made sure to nod my head eagerly. "Prime land would be more than nice. It would be Heaven."

Uncle Blacky shuffled the pages together. "And what will you do to keep them? He has a point about the title and the gun. The Phoenixes would think twice about raiding us if we had those things."

Father's chin sank in toward his chest. Finally he gave a large sigh. "Yes, I suppose you're right. Now guns I know, but what do I say to a magistrate? He'll be a real scholar."

Uncle Blacky stuffed the pages of the letter back into the envelope. "There's nothing to it. I can coach you."

With a sudden smile, Father jerked his head at

Uncle Blacky. "Why not do it yourself, you lazy old fool? I'll buy *you* the title."

"Me?" Uncle Blacky looked as if Father had just told him he was going to become the emperor.

Father used the back of his hand to slap Uncle Blacky's knee. "Let's each fight the battles we're best at."

Uncle Blacky impulsively nodded his head. "For the good of the clan."

I liberated the envelope from Uncle Blacky's hands before he crumpled it in his celebrating. It seemed like a good time to try to keep my promise to Mother by keeping our family together—at least in spirit if not in fact. "Let's not forget the person who made it possible," I reminded them. "We fought and laughed at his dream at every possible chance: and yet he went ahead anyway. And then he was bighearted enough to send us all this money and offer to stay over there as long as we need more."

Father twisted around to face me. "What do you want me to say—that he was right and I was wrong? A hundred mountains of gold couldn't make me do that. And I'm certainly not going to be bribed into that even by this much money."

I took the letter back from Uncle Blacky and slipped it into the envelope. "Well, we at least ought to admit that we were wrong about the golden mountain and he was right." I thought that if I could get Father to make one little concession, I might be able to swing him around gradually into accepting and forgiving Foxfire. After all the trouble I had made for my brother, I thought I owed him that much.

"The future's still here no matter what that fool says. A hundred mountains of gold wouldn't change my mind on that." There was something about Father's tone of voice that told me to be quiet. I thought that I could detect a trace of fear beneath his stubbornness—though of what, I couldn't say. But it was almost as if he had his back to the wall and was making one last stand. Until I knew what he was afraid of, it was useless to argue.

In the meantime, I comforted myself with the knowledge that Father was going to accept some of Foxfire's more practical suggestions; and that was a start toward reconciling the two of them. Mother had said that sometimes you had to nurse your hopes as carefully as you would tend a few little embers. If you kept at it, you could fan them higher and higher into true flames.

Chapter Twenty

For the next ten days, it was almost like a festival in Three Willows. Like some pampered pet, the tale of the golden mountain flourished and grew until it was almost unrecognizable. To hear the others tell it, a guest of the golden mountain only had to put out his hand and the golden nuggets would come rolling down the slope into his palm. Others planned to go overseas.

Remembering what the coolie had said, I tried to warn people about the voyage. But they seemed to think I was trying to protect my brother by scaring away any competition for the gold. They reasoned that if a daydreaming fool like Foxfire could make so much money, then a truly clever person ought to do twice as well.

In the end, six young men decided to try their fortunes overseas. I couldn't help comparing their departure to the way Foxfire had left the village. Instead of having to sneak away, they were seen off by a gathering of the entire clan. Lean, almost skeletal villagers stood up in their field, skull-like heads grinning wolfishly as they wished the travelers good luck.

"He's going to send me a basketful of nuggets," Uncle Windy called.

"They'll each be as big as this." Sticks held a fist over his head and there was a roar of approval. With a little skip and a shuffle, Sticks led the way as jauntily as a general in some opera, and the others swaggered along behind him like heroes out to conquer the world. Then the clan began rising from the fields to pat them on the backs and wish them luck. As a result, the travelers could make their way only slowly toward the valley mouth. When it became impossible to get near the travelers, the latecomers kept a parallel pace along on the other dikes—as if everyone had decided to escort them as far as the mouth of our valley.

But I'd had my fill of such nonsense. We might

all come from the earth of the valley, as Mother had said; but sometimes some "lumps of dirt" seemed much denser than myself. So I decided to get away from them. And my mind naturally turned to Mother. It had been several weeks since I had visited her up at the cemetery.

I went to the three willows that grew near the bank of the stream. They were said to be the three sisters of the First One. The first green buds had appeared on their slender branches and I broke off a few so I could decorate Mother's grave. It was a time when I could talk to Mother about things that were bothering me. Oh, I knew she couldn't answer back. But it gave me a chance to think about things. Sometimes I felt as if I had climbed onto a wild horse on top of a steep mountain; and all I could do was cling to its back while it galloped madly down the steep paths.

When I went back to the village, I found Father still inside the house with the demon gun he had purchased just two days ago.

Long and slender, it was an odd device with two metal barrels. Unlike our matchlocks that ended in a handle you gripped in the right hand, this gun had a triangular-shaped wedge of wood that rested against the right shoulder.

Instead of loading the muzzle like a matchlock, Father worked a lever so that the demon gun broke in half, allowing a cylindrical cartridge to be placed in each barrel. The cartridge contained not only the powder charge but the lead ball as well. Father would then line up the pins at the bases of the cartridges with the notches in the barrels and snap the barrels back onto the wooden stock. He was all ready to shoot in a fraction of the time it took to load the matchlock.

Nor did he need a clumsy burning cord to light the gun. For each barrel there was a dragon-headed piece of metal that would fall on the pin, setting off the charge. And to fire the gun, Father did not press a button as he would on a matchlock. Instead, he pulled at one of the two tonguelike metal slivers.

To me, the demon gun spoke of an entirely different world from ours—an artifact snatched from some other time and place to live for a while in Three Willows. And the gun stank—stank of the dark, sulfurous, strange places within the earth. I would not have been surprised had the demon gun vanished overnight to go back to wherever and whenever it had come from. It just didn't seem to belong in our ancient human world.

"Where are you going?" Father asked when I took

the spatula from the stove. I would use it as a trowel to help clean the grave.

I held up the willow springs. "I thought I'd tend Mother's grave."

Father gave the barrels one last polish with a cloth. "It's been a while since I've been up there." He got up from one of our new benches and slung the pouch of cartridges over one shoulder. "I could always start my patrol from there."

Outside the gates, we could see the clan moving over the dike tops like so many ants scurrying over a lattice. "I hope Sticks and the others make it."

Father shouldered his gun. "On a journey that long, they'll need all the luck they can get."

We trudged on among the fruit trees until we reached the very edge of the orchard. "Wait a moment," Father whispered, and crouched down. "I don't hear any birds. Someone must be there." His eyes searched the pine trees that marked the line of the ridge. They looked like green explosions with their thick branches and long, sharp needles.

I glanced behind me at the village below, but the guard in the tower was watching the parade down on the valley floor, so he wouldn't have seen me signaling. And in the general commotion, I doubt if he would have heard me. "Let's go get help." I said softly.

"We're not sure who or what is there. It might only be some animal." But Father thumbed back the hammers of the gun as he continued to study the shadows under the pine trees.

I stared at him in surprise. "You want a fight so you can use that thing." I pointed at his shotgun.

"This is neither the time nor the place to argue with me." Father waved me back toward the village. Then, still bent over, he slowly shuffled toward the pine trees.

I wasn't sure what to do, so I just stood there. Perhaps it was only an animal, as he suggested, and we would both look foolish for calling out the militia. On the other hand, if it was an ambush, he might need someone to help him. At the very least, he might need my two good legs to go running back for help.

As Father's dark clothes blended into the dense stand of trees, I threw down my basket and started after him. "I'm coming along," I whispered.

About four meters into the trees, Father was waiting for me with an exasperated look. He slapped his palm at the air and I slowed, trying to move on tiptoe over the fragrant pine needles. "Keep five paces behind me," he warned in a low voice.

I stayed where I was until Father was five steps ahead of me and then I began to walk after him.

When Father reached the cemetery, he straightened up. "Get off that grave," he ordered angrily. I hurried behind him and saw that Dusty was sitting on top of a small stone marker only three meters away from us. With his shoulders hunched in his usual way, he looked like a giant vulture waiting for his next meal, so I didn't like the way he eyed Father.

"I was wondering when you were going to come strolling by," Dusty said to Father. When Father began to check the trees for signs of the Phoenixes, Dusty gave a laugh. "You don't have to worry. I'm here all alone." He pointed to the small bundle near his feet and next to it his sword sheathed in a scabbard with a baldric—a strap that could be hung over one shoulder. "I've parted ways with the Phoenixes. They're all idiots."

Father kept the gun barrels aimed at Dusty. "So they fired you."

Dusty seemed determined not to take any offense. "I was their guest," he corrected Father patiently. "And when they wouldn't listen to my advice, I decided to leave."

"What sort of advice?" Father stepped out into the light so he could stand up.

"I told them at the very start that they ought to send someone to investigate the golden mountain. But they couldn't see why they should change their recipe for success, because it's always worked so well in the past." Dusty crossed his legs. "Now it's too late. Your clan is on the rise. But"—he inclined his head to the side meaningfully—"your clan could climb even faster with *my* help."

"We've done well enough without you." Father tightened his grip on his gun.

"But you're not aggressive enough. You could grind the Phoenixes under your heels. I could tell you how." In his eagerness, he uncrossed his legs and rose to his feet.

"Stay back," Father warned him.

"Or what?" Dusty's eyes narrowed.

"Or this." Father brought the gun up to his shoulder. Cringing, Dusty ducked; but Father had already swung the barrels slightly to the right, his shoulder leaning into the gun. His finger pulled one trigger and the gun bucked like a living thing in his hands. There was a bright flash of light and then a cloud of smoke. Branches of a nearby tree snapped and went crashing to the ground.

Father swung the gun back to Dusty again. "That was just a warning. I think this makes us equal in a fight now. So I suggest that you pick up your things and leave, since you don't like the neighborhood anymore."

"You're an even bigger fool than the Phoenixes. What's the good of holding power if you won't use it?" He began to scratch the back of his head vigorously as if Father truly irritated him. "You ought to give that gun to someone who will use it properly."

"How can you have peace in the land if you can't have peace within yourself?" Father quoted a saying of Mother's.

Suddenly Dusty snatched something from his collar and whipped the object at Father. Father pulled the trigger, but he was too late. Dusty had already thrown himself low to the side. The pellets of the shotgun blast rattled and chipped the grave markers.

And then Father gave a cry. I turned in horror to see that what Dusty had flung at Father was a throwing dagger—a slim triangle of iron about as long and as wide as my index finger. Its base now sat in the flesh of Father's arm. Even as I watched, a red spot began to spread outward from the dagger and Father's legs buckled in his pain. The gun barrels slammed against the earth.

Dusty had rolled two meters farther on. He looked up with a wolfish smile when he saw Father on his knees. "Did you forget Canton so soon? We were always able to take guns from the demons—if we were willing to risk our lives."

Chapter Twenty-One

Dusty confidently slipped another throwing dagger from his sleeve. In his own mind, the gun was as good as his. "It's a pity you didn't accept my earlier offer. I would have shared power with you."

Father managed to work the lever with just one hand so that the gun barrels swung downward on their hinge and away from the stock.

"Is that how you do it?" Dusty sauntered toward Father insolently, knowing he could still get Father before the gun could be loaded.

I would have traded all the gold on Foxfire's mountain for a little more time—just enough for

Father to get a cartridge from his pouch, put it into the barrel and then line up the pin at the base of the cartridge so that it fit into the notch of the barrel. With two hands, Father could do it almost as fast as I could describe it. But he only had one good hand now.

He laid the barrels across his knees, holding them there with his bad arm while his right hand dug into his pouch. Dusty was already raising the throwing dagger over his head for a fatal toss.

Well, I may not have had a mountain of gold, but perhaps I could still buy a few precious moments for Father. "Dusty," I yelled and threw the willow twigs and then the spatula—more in hopes of distracting then of hitting him.

I saw with a certain satisfaction that Dusty had thrown himself to the ground. Even as the spatula thumped against the dirt, I charged forward. "The Youngs. The Youngs," I shouted.

"Why, you little hellcat." Dusty was already rising to his hands and knees.

I planted my foot and kicked at him with all my might. But I'd been too eager and tried to kick him too soon. Though I had my leg stretched out as far as I could, my foot still missed his head. But when

I kicked, it flung up a huge cloud of dust. It wasn't tournament rules, but I didn't care. Bringing my foot down, I kicked up even more dust.

Suddenly Dusty stumbled into the clear, coughing and rubbing at his eyes. He stopped short when he came up against a grave marker.

While he was temporarily blinded, I threw myself at his stomach. It felt as hard as a board when my shoulder hit it, but both of us fell on top of someone's grave.

My hands grabbed his wrist and cracked it against a grave marker so that he dropped the throwing dagger. Then I tried to use some of the blows and holds Father had shown me; but Dusty had already recovered from his surprise. Blind as he was, his superior strength and knowledge let him toss me easily to the side as if I were only a little doll.

"Get away from him," I heard Father shout. I rolled and then scrambled to my feet, half expecting to feel him grab my ankle, but he missed.

I heard the click now of the shotgun barrels being snapped back into place. I had been annoyed by the noise before when Father had been practicing loading his gun. But there wasn't a more welcome sound on the earth at that moment. I circled away among the markers to give Father a wide berth.

I couldn't help wondering, though, if it was wise to shoot the shotgun. I remembered how the barrels had hit the earth when Father had been wounded at first. Father had been very fussy about keeping the barrels clean, saying that if dirt got into the barrels, it could block the charge and perhaps make the gun explode in his hands.

Father had managed to raise his left arm enough for the barrels to rest on his forearm. "Hold it right there."

Dusty lay still as the air cleared from our little tussle. He wiped at his eyes. "I didn't know you could load so fast with just one hand.'

"There are a lot of thing you don't know—like loyalty and honor." Father pulled back the hammers. "We were comrades once, so I'll let you go. But don't ever show your face around here again."

Dusty blinked his eyes, as if he were just managing to see again. "If we equipped just thirty men with guns like that, we could—"

"I like things as they are." Father held the gun steady. "We'll have peace, in our valley at least."

"The king of a dungheap," Dusty said scornfully as he sat up.

"It's a big enough kingdom for us." Father adjusted the barrels' aim ever so slightly. "And we don't intend to be bullied ever again."

"So there's no longer any profit here for your kind." I stepped around among the markers until I came to his things. Using the baldric to tie the sword hilt to the scabbard, I tossed his weapon over to him. When I listed up his bundle, I heard jingling and clinking. I felt it cautiously, but there weren't any sharp points so I didn't think it held any throwing daggers.

The bundle seemed to contain objects that were more like cash and jewelry. Well, the Phoenixes had only themselves to blame if Dusty had stolen things from them. I swung the bundle through the air so that it landed next to his sheathed sword.

Dusty cautiously picked up his bundle and sword. "It won't end here," he swore.

Father, however, was not frightened. He had a promise of his own. "Then you'd better pick a spot for your grave now, because if I see you near my valley again, you're a dead man."

Dusty gave us an angry, frustrated look and retreated into the trees. We could hear his soft steps fading away quickly. Father kept his gun balanced on his arm until he was sure he was away. Then the barrels sagged to the ground and his left shoulder drooped.

His wounded arm was soaked with blood now; but he worried about his gun first, lowering the hammers onto the loaded barrel before he set it down on the ground. "What a team we make," he exulted. "I almost think we could take on the demons and the Manchus right now."

Thinking that this was my big chance, I knelt beside Father. "Don't forget Foxfire. He helped make it possible."

Father winced, but I couldn't have said whether it was from the dagger in his arm or the thought of his son. "You don't give up, do you?"

I began to tear a strip of cloth from the bottom of my blouse to use as a tourniquet. "Of course not— I'm your daughter." I added, "And Foxfire is your son. He sent the money because he cares about us, not to prove a point to you."

Father gripped the base of the dagger. "But you remember his letter. He still thinks the Work is a lie."

I wound the strip of cloth around his arm. "It's possible to love someone even if you don't agree with him."

Father yanked the dagger from his arm and held up the bloody little triangle. "I suppose that's true."

I finished tying the knot. "Of course it is."

"What's the use?" Father threw the dagger away and it clinked against someone's stone marker. "I mean, let's say I did acknowledge him again. How would he know? My lungs aren't strong enough to shout the news all that way across the ocean."

It was the moment I had been waiting for. "I've been thinking about it for the last few days. Why don't we write him?" I hardly dared to believe my own boldness, but I plunged on anyway. I might lack Mother's abilities, but at least I could imitate her persistence. "We could dictate a letter to Uncle Blacky."

Father jerked his head back as if I had just tried to bite off his nose. "Foxfire's friend apparently isn't a man of great learning. But you can hardly expect a scholar like Uncle Blacky to write down our . . . well, our common thoughts as if they were something special."

I was all prepared for that argument too. "He's so kindhearted that I honestly don't think he'd mind; but even if he did, he still owes you a favor for buying that title for him." I settled back on my heels.

"I'm ready for any excuse you might try to use."

Father picked up his gun as if that could somehow inspire him. "Cassia, try to understand. I'm grateful to that boy—well, I suppose I should really call him a man now—who's named Foxfire. But he's wrong about the Work. Our future is here. His future should be here."

As I got up to retrieve my spatula, I realized that getting Father to forgive Foxfire was going to be a far more difficult task than beating Dusty. "Did you ever stop and think he might need some encouragement?"

Father looked as if he were torn between his own faith in the Work and his love for his son. "Well," he compromised, "what you do with Uncle Blacky is your own business—even if it's to send a note overseas."

My eyes searched Father's face. "But don't you want to say anything?"

"I'm willing to give in on any point but the Work. Until he realizes the truth about the Revolution, he's no child of mine." Father began to stump back toward the village.

I sighed as I followed Father. No matter what Father thought, he and Foxfire had one thing in common. They were both so proud that they could give lessons to statues in being stiff-necked. But at least I had made a start.

I glanced at the marker on Mother's grave. "I'm trying," I whispered to her. "But it's hard." And then I followed Father back to the village.

Chapter Twenty-Two

Father refused to add anything to my first letter to Foxfire. And though I worked on him steadily during the next four months, I couldn't get him to change his mind—despite all the good things that Foxfire was making possible.

With money borrowed against Foxfire's payments, I had purchased three prime fields from the Golden Cat. With sufficient water and plenty of fertilizer, I was looking forward to the best summer crop I'd ever had. And if things went the way I planned, I'd be able to tell Foxfire that we didn't need his money. That way he could pay off his debts in less than three years. Then he could come home to receive the recognition he deserved. I didn't think even Father could resist forgiving Foxfire if his son were here in the flesh. Though I hadn't been the best of big sisters in the past, I was determined to do right by him now.

All around me, our rice plants were "drawing starch," as they say, and turning a golden color as they ripened in the sun. A breeze swept across the valley, and I watched the rice plants bend their heads and then rise. The ripples spread outward across my fields as if I were at the heart of a pool of golden light.

It had only been a little less than a year since I had wished that I might have fields like these. What a difference time and money could make. Almost nostalgically, I returned to the field where Mother had died. I'd bought that one cheap from the Golden Cat and turned it to growing leeks, a good cash crop. I could expect to take some sixteen harvests from each plant, and each harvest might sell for six times what the rice would. But I'd never had the extra money for the equipment or the additional fertilizer they required until I had hired Aster and Tiny.

Aster was in the field, watering each plant by hand. "They're thirsty little things, aren't they?" It had been necessary to pay a few bribes to increase our water ration.

I crossed the deep ditch filled with water and examined the long leaves of one plant. We had covered the plants with tubular tiles so they would bleach the way people liked—though Aster had taken off the tiles to water the leeks. "I think these leaves are ready to cut. Do you want to take some?"

"Sure. If you'll take some of my eggplants. I just harvested some." Aster pointed over to a basket by the ditch. The money I paid her helped her to buy fertilizer, seed and water for her own field, so she and Tiny were doing well themselves.

I walked over to the basket and began to sort through them. I'd never seen fatter, more colorful eggplants, and the curves of one just seemed to fit naturally into my palm. I turned with the eggplant in my hand. "It's like being in a fairy tale."

"Well, you've been touched by magic, haven't you? If an outsider came into this valley, he could pick out all the guest families." "Guest families" is what the clan called any family who had sent a man overseas. "You're stronger, healthier." She gestured with a long-handled dipper toward my hips. "Fatter. It's almost as if you were a different race."

"We're just eating better." I touched a corner of my mouth. "The canker sores heal now instead of festering on and on."

Disgusted, Aster went on watering the plants. "Poetical images are lost on you."

The sound of hammering floated down the side of the valley. That would be the carpenters building extra rooms for Uncle Windy. Though the other families had been more cautious because their money had not begun to arrive yet, Uncle Windy had already borrowed heavily against the day when it would come. "Well, someone's even getting a palace like they do in fairy tales." I couldn't help laughing.

Aster joined in quickly enough. Despite the poor rainfall this season, the laughter seemed to come easily to everyone now. And it was really all Foxfire's doing.

I cradled the eggplant against my stomach. "I really misjudged my brother, didn't I? I should have realized that this place was too small for someone with dreams like his."

Aster lowered the dipper into the ditch and left it there for a moment. "Oh, now don't start that again," she scolded me. "We all thought his schemes were crazy."

I sat down. "I wonder if some of his other notions

might be more practical than I originally thought." And I told her about his plan to keep the seed from the best plants in order to develop healthier and bigger crops.

Aster dragged the dipper back and forth in the ditch. "Well, why not experiment with the seed from one field?"

I kicked my heel thoughtfully against the dirt and then gave a slight shake of my head. "I'm not sure that's what Mother would have done."

"I thought you would've outgrown that kind of talk, Cassia," Aster scolded. "You've accomplished just as much in these four months as she would have—maybe even more."

Agreeing with her would have sounded like false pride to me; but before I could say anything, I felt the breeze freshen and blow stronger. "Did you feel that?"

Aster raised the dipper in both hands. "It's only the wind."

"But it feels moist." I looked back toward my new rice fields, knowing how vulnerable they were at this point. If heavy rains came now, the water would cause the kernels of rice to sprout on the stalks, ruining the entire crop. But it was still to early to harvest them.

"You're worrying too much," Aster tried to assure me. "The rains have all been light this season."

"I suppose you're right." I got to my feet again. "It's just that we've borrowed so much money that I can't afford to lose any of the crop."

Had I been so eager to please Foxfire, Father and the others that I had let myself spend more money than I should have? Besides buying our new fields, Father's gun and Uncle Blacky's title, we had had to pay bribes to the bandits and help replace the house that was lost during the bandit raid. Father had insisted on giving food to his militiamen to keep them from starving. And then I'd been so eager to make us rich so Foxfire could come home. Would Mother have risked letting us get into such a financial mess? I didn't think so. I started to panic.

"That's what comes of having a conscience. They're very expensive things." Aster poured the water from the dipper onto a plant. "But quit fretting. Everything will be fine."

As I tended the leeks, I tried to follow Aster's advice; but I couldn't help casting anxious looks at the narrow gray clouds that drifted overhead like so many lazy dragons. "It looks like a storm," I said finally.

She didn't even bother glancing up. "This season there have been plenty of clouds that have passed over the valley without raining."

But even Aster ran out of optimistic things to say by the later afternoon. A wind began to roar across the fields, pouncing now here, now there like a playful tiger. It tugged and pulled at my hat so the ribbons I used for tying it to my head cut into my chin. By the end of the day a purple sheet of clouds covered the sky, casting a terrible gloom over everything.

I could feel the darkness spreading into me as well. "Aster, I don't like the look of things."

With an anxious glance up at the sky, Aster motioned me to stay where I was. "Let me take care of everything."

I watched as she picked up her basket of eggplants and walked quickly across the fields and up the path toward the village. She returned shortly with an umbrella. I stared at it, because I could see all the holes in the coated parchment. "What do you want with that old thing?"

"Treat this umbrella with more respect." Aster playfully opened the umbrella as she stood on the dike. If anything, the umbrella was now more hole than parchment. "It's going to jinx the storm," she explained. "It never rains when I remember to bring this thing along."

Rain on coated parchment makes an unmistakable loud sound—like a tap of a stick on a small drum. We both stiffened when we heard it now.

"No," I murmured.

"It's just a stray drop," Aster tried to assure me, but the smile was gone from her face.

Tip-tap-tip.

"A *few* stray drops," I added, and then gave a cry when raindrops fell one after another on my sleeve. They seemed to burn like acid.

All around us, people were rising in alarm. But the tapping only increased to a loud rattling; and the raindrops fell from the sky like miniature arrows. I watched as the dry, drained soil began to turn a rich, black color. And the rice plants deepened with moisture until they were almost a deadly golden brown.

Aster shook her umbrella. "You're not doing your job."

I gathered up my things. "Come on. We'd better get back to the village."

Aster held out her umbrella so I could share it. "Here."

I pointed to all the holes. "I'll get just as wet with

that thing as without." I slipped on the wet soil as I climbed out of the field.

Aster caught my arm before I fell over. With her help I pulled myself up beside her. "Don't worry," she had to shout as the water poured on down. "This storm will go away now that it's seen this." And she gave her umbrella a forlorn shake.

Father was waiting for me anxiously when I got home. "How bad is it?"

"If the rain keeps up, we could lose the rice crop." I picked up a clean rag and began to polish the table and benches we'd bought three months ago. If times go hard again, I thought I might be able to sell them for a few cash.

In his nervousness, he began to pull at the base of his queue. "Can we borrow enough money to cover our losses?"

"The interest rates on a second loan would be ruinous. We'd find ourselves so deeply in debt that we might never be able to get out of it." I wadded up the cleaning rag in one hand. "I haven't kept any kind of money reserve. I had to show everyone just how smart we were. I've borrowed money to buy the fields and fertilizer and seed and water. And then there were the bribes we had to pay to the bandits and the clan elders."

"And Uncle Blacky's title. And the help we gave my militiamen." Father sat down heavily on one of the benches. "I . . . I didn't know we had that many debts."

"I was stupid." I struck the knuckles of my free hand against my forehead. "I was so busy showing off to the clan that I didn't keep anything back for bad times."

Father grabbed my hand so I couldn't strike myself anymore. "Why didn't you tell me before?"

"I wanted to help you just like Mother did: run the household and the fields . . . or at least keep the family together. But all I've managed to do was make a complete mess of everything." I shook my head in utter misery. "I don't know whatever made me think I could take Mother's place."

Father squeezed my hand. "But it's not your fault, child. It's mine. I asked you to spend all that money."

The tears began to slip down my cheeks. "I should have had the good sense not to do it. Mother would have."

"You've done your best," Father said in his most encouraging voice. "And that's all anyone could ask."

I swept the rag across my eyes, but the tears just kept on coming. "And my best hasn't been good enough. Mother would never have botched things like this."

"I've been meaning to talk to you about this for a long time." Father patted one of the benches. "Sit down."

"But I should begin cooking." I started to turn toward the stove.

"SIT DOWN," Father barked in his drillmaster's voice. Though he used that sort of voice outside in the courtyard when he was instructing me, I couldn't recall his ever using that tone inside the house. Surprised, I plopped down right on the spot he had indicated. "Yes?"

Father swung a leg over the bench so he was now straddling it. "You're not your mother; and no one expects you to be."

My palms began to ache, and I realized that worry had made me twist the rag until it was as thin and hard as a rope. "But I should be. I have to be."

Father ran a hand over his head while he chose his words with great care. "You're not doing such a bad job either."

"No?" I sniffed. I laid the rag down on the table, where it began to uncoil.

Father slid a strong, reassuring arm around my

shoulders. "And she would have been the first one to tell you that. She would have preferred you to be yourself." He gave me a little shake. "You're your own person with your own way of living and your own dreams. Come out from underneath her shadow."

Half blinded by tears now, I could only see Father as a kind of blur. "Do you really mean that?"

I thought he held up a hand. "I swear on my honor. Your mother would never have wanted to haunt you this way."

It was funny, but I suddenly felt the strangest sense of relief—as if Father had lifted a huge load of thorns from my back. All I wanted to do was hide my face against his shirt and have a good long cry. And that's what I did. Father began to rock me back and forth as he had when I was small.

After a while, he gripped my arms and made me sit up straight. "You'll manage. I know you will."

"I suppose you're right." I tried wiping my eyes again, and this time the tears stopped.

"Of course I'm right." He winked at me. "And the rain will stop soon enough. You'll see."

But though Father was a man with a brave, good heart, he was no prophet.

The rain continued to fall all that night.

Chapter Twenty-Three

Even though it was still raining the next morning, I went slogging through the mud to inspect our fields. I wanted to race to the first field, but the mud was so thick that it clung to my legs. It was all I could do to pull my feet free every time I tried to take a step. And the other people had to struggle just as hard to move through the soggy desolation. And I could only think of insects caught in paste.

People were already weeping in the nearby fields, and when I got to the nearest one of mine, I found that the rice was already beginning to sprout on the stalk. I tried to hurry on to the next; but I could only struggle along slowly—all the time telling myself that it would be different in the next field. But it was the same in that field and all the others. We'd lost the entire first rice crop.

I saved the leeks for last, making my way with difficulty over to the spot where Mother had died. I kept my eyes away from the crop itself, turning them instead toward the trees on the ridge line. The falling rain made them seem like black shapes glimpsed dimly through smoke. Mother had said the view might have made that ancestor feel fresh and new. But with every step, I felt as if I were now fighting the earth itself as it tried to suck me down.

It was only when I was on the edge of the ditch that I dared to look down. It was even worse than I had thought. The cash crop upon which I had based so many plans looked as if it were drowning. I couldn't expect many of the plants to survive.

Despite the mud, I sank to my knees. I just couldn't take it anymore. I was tired of dreaming, scheming, fighting. Foxfire had been right. The earth here was old and tired. I had been the one who had been fooling myself. I looked around the valley and suddenly felt as weary and worn out as its soil.

But as I knelt there, trying to think of what to do, I could hear people talking in their fields. The only ones who could speak confidently of the future were those families whose men were guests of the land of the golden mountain. In the midst of their weeping and moaning, other families were considering sending someone overseas. Whether they actually took the risk or not, the golden mountain was something that gave them new hope in the middle of their misery—like people trapped inside a black cave who suddenly see a little pinpoint of light. It was strange to hear how often and how respectfully everyone mentioned Foxfire.

My little brother had found more respect than Father had with a lifetime of fighting. It was just a shame that Foxfire couldn't hear some of the compliments. But he really wouldn't have cared. That wasn't his way. It was a shame that he had to go so far away before I began to appreciate his better qualities. I'd wanted him to come home because I missed his company. And then he could be safe and have the honor that was due him from everyone, including myself. Unfortunately, it wasn't going to be much of a homecoming now—not unless we postponed it long enough for us to get back on our feet.

And I was torn between what I knew had to be done and bringing my little brother home. I had thought about it and thought about it all last night while I had listened to the rain. But I could come up with only one solution.

When I got back to our house, I discovered Father had used our fuel recklessly in order to get a good fire roaring in the stove. The dry heat enveloped me in a reassuring wave as I came through the door. I closed my eyes almost blissfully, for I'd been feeling like a muddy rat up to that moment. The water dripped from my cloak of rice straw and hat, the drops pattering noisily onto our floor.

"Is it very bad?" Father sounded as if he were preparing himself for the worst.

"People are saying that this is the worst storm they can remember." I shed my rain gear, leaving it by the doorway. Despite the cloak and hat, I'd gotten drenched to the skin. "We've lost the entire rice crop. And probably the leeks too."

In his nervousness, Father twisted a handful of rice straw so that it made crisp, crackling sounds. "I know how to deal with Manchus and Phoenixes, but how do I fight miserable weather like this?"

I went over to the stove and held out my arms, watching the steam rise from my sleeves like little ghosts. "I can think of only one way out for us; but you won't like it."

He threw the rice straw into the opening. "Try me."

I lowered my arms. "I think the interest rates would be better over in the land of the golden mountain, so perhaps we should write a second letter and ask Foxfire to borrow some money and send it to us. I can probably stall our creditors long enough." I hunched my shoulders, bracing myself for an angry explosion.

But Father only looked away. "How much longer would he have to spend overseas?"

I lowered my shoulders. "I don't know. It might add another four or five years. Maybe even more."

Father gave a start. "That long?"

I stepped around so he had to face me again. "We ought to give him his choice, of course; but I think I already know what his answer would be. After all, he offered to stay as long as we needed." I waved a hand toward the box where we kept Foxfire's letters. "And this time our fields will come first. I'll be careful with the way I manage his money."

"But I hate to tell him how badly we failed." Father clasped his hands behind his back anxiously.

I grabbed Father's arm. "I don't like asking this any more than you do. But what's he got to come home to now? We've got nothing. In fact, we're worse off than before."

"I still don't know if we have the right to ask him to stay."

"He's fighting the war he wants to fight," I said. "You heard him yourself. He thinks the real enemy is poverty, not the Manchus. He's fighting the war he thinks ought to be fought."

"I wish he'd shown half as much determination and courage for the Work," he sighed.

I pressed my thumbs into his arm—not hard enough to hurt but firm enough to emphasize my words. "Why should he fight our war?"

Father used his free hand to scratch his cheek in irritation. "What do you mean?"

I licked my lips nervously, feeling like someone about to make a risky move in a fight. "You said yesterday that I didn't have to be like Mother. So why should Foxfire have to be exactly like you?"

"I did say that, didn't I?" he said grudgingly.

I knew I had him now. "It's not good advice unless you can follow it yourself. He's coming home eventually—maybe not after three years now, but some-

[258]

time. What are you going to do then? Hide in the hills? Ignore him?"

He laughed sadly. "I can see that I'm never going to have a moment's peace until I give in."

"It's the serpent's blood in me," I reminded him. "Once I sink my fangs in, I never let go."

"Sometimes I don't know whether that's good or bad." He smiled ruefully.

"I know it's hard to swallow your pride," I tried to coax him, "but you've always been able to make difficult choices before this. Why don't you admit you were wrong? Acknowledge Foxfire as your son. He might need the encouragement."

Father frowned. "It sounds like I've let him buy my forgiveness."

"Foxfire knows you better than that." I jerked my head at Father. "At least put something in my next letter to him."

Father stared at the stove for a long time. The waves of heat made its shape seem to waver as if it were only an illusion. "This is not the way I would have made up with Foxfire. But you're right. If I'm going to ask him to spend even more years overseas, I ought to tell him that he is my son—even if I don't always understand him . . . or his wild notions."

Suddenly we could hear the shouting from outside. "What now?" Father started for the door, but I motioned him to stay inside.

"There's no sense for both of us to get wet. Let me find out what it is." And putting on my rain gear again, I headed outside.

Despite the rain, there was a little knot of people in front of Uncle Windy's house when we entered the lane.

"But Sticks was young and strong," Uncle Windy was protesting.

"Sometimes the stronger they are, the less chance they have on the ships. The fevers seem to hit those men first, or they get into a fight. . . ." The clerk shrugged. "At any rate, you must pay off all your debts."

"We . . . we have nothing." Uncle Windy glanced helplessly at his wife and then spread out his hands.

"What about your fields?" The clerk scratched his temple.

"We're still paying on them." Aunt Piety dropped to her knees and pressed her forehead against the earth. "Please have mercy on us."

"Your house?" The clerk gestured toward it.

"Mortgaged. We tried to borrow against the money

we expected, but that didn't cover all the construction." Uncle Windy copied his wife and knelt on the ground. "We have nothing."

The clerk held up a hand. "Now take it easy. I don't really want you. There's a glut of people on the market right now. I would rather have cold, hard cash. Can't you borrow any money?"

Uncle Windy looked up, his face a picture of absolute misery. Dirt now mixed with the tears to send muddy streaks coursing down his cheeks. "No, I—" Suddenly his eyes caught sight of me. "Cassia. Please help us."

Though I didn't exactly like my uncle, I wouldn't wish that fate on anyone. So my first inclination was to say yes. But I thought again about how much we had borrowed ourselves. And I felt like a swimmer who is rising toward the surface. She can see the light just above her, perhaps even feel the dryness of the air on her hands as they break through the surface. And suddenly other people grab hold of her legs as if they expect her to pull them up as well.

We were already helping far too many people as it was. If I let myself get caught now, other families whose sons or husbands did not survive would also ask us for money.

I took several steps back. "I'm sorry, Uncle. But I tried to tell you what the coolie said."

"Yes, yes, and I should have listened, but I was a fool. A fool." Uncle Windy started to crawl forward on his hands and knees when the clerk motioned to two of his coolies to grab him. "Cassia, don't hold the foot binding against me. Please." Then he couldn't say anything else, because his face had been shoved into the dirt so they could bind his hands behind his back.

Aunt Piety straightened so she could hold out her hands to me. "Cassia," she begged, "don't be hardhearted. Forget what we did to you in the past. Didn't I try to be kind?" Two other coolies took the opportunity to seize her wrists and bind them.

I turned desperately to the clerk. "There were others who went with Sticks. They didn't all die, did they?"

The clerk consulted a list in his hand. "Three men survived from this village."

"That many died?" Those were even more deaths than the coolie had predicted.

"It depends on the ship. Some voyages no one dies." The clerk folded up his list. "The stakes are high in this game."

"But what about the other two families?" I had

to know the worst. "Are you going to claim them too?"

"No, they owe us only for the passage money, and we have their houses and fields as security." The clerk drew the list back and forth between his fingers. "Your uncle and aunt are the only ones who really need help."

"What about the new guest families?" I suggested.

"I'll ask them," the clerk shrugged, "but I rather suspect they'll say the same thing. You're in a better position than they are." From the bored way he spoke, it seemed as if he had been through this same scene before.

Uncle Windy struggled against the grip of the coolies and somehow managed to raise his head so he could speak again. "You really are nothing but a mean, spiteful little snake. You've never forgotten and you've never forgiven. Well, this moment will come back to you."

The tears began to roll down my cheeks. "Uncle, Aunty, I'd like to help you if I could. I really would." I looked around at the rest of the clan. "Honestly, I would."

But from the scowls on the faces of the others, I knew they didn't believe me any more than Uncle Windy did. He spat at me and then turned his face toward Heaven. "Listen to me. Let her come to a time when she has to beg, and may people be just as deaf." Before Uncle Windy could add anything more to the curse, the coolies wrestled him to the mud again.

I started to back toward my house, but the clerk slipped an envelope from his sleeve. "Wait. Don't go. I have a letter for you." From one large sleeve of his robe, he took a flat rectangle wrapped in oil-cloth.

Since we banked Foxfire's remittances in town to cover our debts, we weren't actually expecting money; but we did get letters faithfully from Foxfire. "Th-thank you," I stammered.

"It's my job," the clerk said as he glanced down impatiently. "Finish tying up his hands. I want to be back in town before night fall."

With a nervous look at the sky, I retreated into my courtyard. Would Uncle Windy's fate be ours as well? Why had I spent so much money?

Fear made my stomach tighten and brought a dry-ness to my throat. And I began to wonder if the White Serpent had felt this way just before the priest had destroyed all her magical illusions. Our own dreams and plans were dissolving almost as quickly.

Chapter Twenty-Four

Father was standing in the doorway with a horrified expression on his face. "Can't we do something for Uncle Windy?" He'd overheard everything, I suppose.

I held up the letter. "We'll be lucky to save ourselves." I felt ashamed, in a way, because I was sure Mother would have tried to do something. But Father had said that I had to do things my way—and I was.

Father took a deep breath and then let it out slowly. "I'll go get Uncle Blacky."

I shoved past Father. Even if I didn't like Uncle

Windy, I didn't like abandoning him this way. "Then I'll heat the wine."

I had just finished changing to a dry set of clothes when Father returned with Uncle Blacky. I could hear the clan calling questions to them in the lane, but both of them refused to talk until they were safely within our courtyard. "It's a terrible business about the voyagers," Uncle Blacky said as he stepped into our house.

Father followed him a moment later, settling Uncle Blacky's umbrella against the wall by the doorway. "Let's not stand on ceremony tonight. I'm afraid my curiosity's gotten the better of me."

Uncle Blacky sat down in his usual spot. "Well, I think we're all wondering what the young fellow might have to say." He nodded a greeting to me as I busied myself about the stove.

Father got the letter himself and placed it before Uncle Blacky. "It's kind of you to indulge me," he said, sitting down on the other side of the table.

"Don't give it another thought." Uncle Blacky opened the envelope and took out the letter. "Oh, dear. It seems to be more of a scrawl than usual." He squinted at it. "But I suppose they might have been in a hurry." And he began to read the first page, pausing every now and then to figure out a word.

"I didn't want to worry you unnecessarily; but I can see that I was wrong. I must warn you that the voyage over here is not an easy one.

"I think that I have had a little taste of death. The demons crammed hundreds of us into the hold of their ship. I had to stand sideways to squeeze down the aisle between the tiers of sleeping shelves. (We were charged extra for the sleeping shelves, the money being added to our debt. It will take me longer to pay it off now.) And what a lot of dialects! Men calling out for anyone from the Four Districts or from the Three Districts or from the Fragrant Mountain district.

"There the demons locked us into the hold; and as the heat grew worse, men would crouch beneath the hatches in the hope of getting some fresh breeze, but most of the time they were disappointed. And not only was it hot in the hold, but it stank awfully.

"I found out that we were also charged for the water in the tanks that the demons had set up for us, and the demons would not let us fetch sea water so we could wash ourselves as often as we would have liked or to clean out the hold. As a result, we could do nothing when the night-soil pails tipped over and feces and urine ran on the decks or when the vomit ran down the sides of the tiers. Through the interpreter, we were told that a ship had been taken over by pirates who had hidden among the laborers. We told him that we were not pirates. Even so, he said, we must endure the smell. He claimed it was no worse than the fields we fertilize, but he is very wrong.

"I had barely gotten over being seasick when a storm caught our ship. In rough seas, we could not cook. We could only lie on our sleeping shelves and listen to the wind howling. It was dark in the hold except for the light from a few demon oil lanterns. With the ship swaying as it was, the shadows would go twisting and leaping about the walls of the hold as if the world itself were about to come apart. It was then that we found the sleeping shelves were not built well. The tier next to me came apart, and the man on the top shelf fell down on all the men below with a splintering crash. One man broke a leg. We did what we could; but it turned gangrenous and he died.

"Then the demons discovered that some of our barrels of pork had gone bad and salt water had gotten into some of our rice. We listened in dismay as the barrels were tossed over the side. We knew we would be on short rations after that.

"Fights broke out often, for besides everything else, we did not know one another well. Even though we tried to make friends, it was not the same. When men became angry, they did not feel as much shame as they would have at home surrounded by other members of their clan. The gambling games are often a source for fights. Sometimes someone tries to shove ahead in line for something. Sometimes you simply bump into another person. A man in the tier to my left had a heavy pair of boots that he used for a pillow every night. One morning I found him with his throat slit and his boots gone. We left his body beneath the hatch, where the demons could see it and take it away to dump in the sea.

"But the worst part of life in the ship's hold is the boredom. There is very little to do except to gamble, and there are so many cheats that it is wise to stay away from the games. The man on the shelf underneath me brought along a moon guitar. He promised to teach me how to play it, but then he caught a fever. He raved out loud for three days and three nights.

"When I fetched water for him, a bad sort of man, who gambled a lot, shook his head. 'You're wasting water on your friend. He'll be dead soon enough. It's better to save it for the rest of us.'

"And that night I woke to the tier shaking. There were shadowy figures standing on either side of the tier, and I heard one of them shouting at the man below me, 'Be quiet, will you? We need our sleep.' And then I heard choking noises.

"I kicked out at one of them. I missed and the man caught my ankles and pulled me off my shelf, so I fell to the deck and was knocked unconscious. When I woke, the shadows were gone. The other men lay on their shelves pretending to be asleep. I looked at my friend on his shelf and found that he had been strangled. His moon guitar and all his other belongings were gone. So were mine.

"But I have survived. And that is no small boast. Out of every three men who walked down into that hold, only two lived to walk out. Despite that, I never once thought that I was going to die during the voyage. Strange. I numbed myself to any fear. Death was something that took the others. Never me.

"But when we finally reached the demon city and I could climb shakily from the hold, I felt like I was being born again. And then all the numbness left me and I was almost paralyzed by shame and guilt. Why was I alive and the others dead? I tell myself it was fate, but how can I be sure? Perhaps I was the one who was meant to die, but some other man was taken by mistake. Even now, I feel dreadfully ashamed.

"And perhaps that is another reason that I did

not tell you about my trip overseas. However, I do not know if the tragedy could have been averted anyway. My cousins may not have had any choice in trying to reach the land of the Golden Mountain. But only the strong and hardy should attempt to come over; and even then they will be gambling with death.

"Nor is life easy in this violent land. We are often subject to the whims of any demon with a gun. Even the climate can be harsh and cruel for people raised in our warm, southern lands.

"Well, do not worry about my surviving cousins. I have done what I could for them right now. And when the winter comes, I will make sure they have the necessary clothing.

"But I hear from some of the recent arrivals that things have not been easy in the Middle Kingdom. Though I would like to come home as soon as possible, I want you to know that I will stay as long as necessary to make sure that you are both happy and comfortable. I will stay here the rest of my life if that is what you need.

"As always, you are in my thoughts and prayers."

Uncle Blacky held up the last page for us to see. "He's signed it 'The Fool.' "

Father shook his head from side to side. "I didn't

think the boy had it in him to survive a trip like that. Or to live in a place that dangerous."

"And he's willing to stay for the rest of his life," I reminded Father.

He arched his eyebrows. "He never seemed all that strong or capable."

I couldn't help defending Foxfire as I filled their cups with wine. "You said I have to do things my way and not Mother's. Well, maybe Foxfire's finally found the path he wants to take."

"That's true." Uncle Blacky sipped from his cup. "Sometimes it's a question of finding the right place in which to grow. A rosebush in a garden is a lovely thing; but put it in a field and it's simply a weed."

Thinking this was my big chance, I set the wine kettle back on the stove. "But even if he doesn't support the Work, he does care about us. Most other people would have been bragging about how tough they were. But he didn't want to worry us."

Uncle Blacky tossed down his wine. "I think he's earned the right to be called your son again, don't you?"

Father settled back, curling his fingers around his cup. "I keep insulting him; and he keeps forgiving me. And now he's just solved all our money troubles. How can I ignore a boy like that?"

"Forgive me, Father," I said cautiously, "but after everything he's been through he's not a boy anymore, he's a man. After all, he's made his own decision to stay."

Father considered that for a long time and then sighed heavily. "I suppose he . . ." He corrected himself with a slight smile. "That is, my son is a man. I should have realized that long before, but I just didn't want to admit that he was right."

"Right about what?" I asked.

When Father spoke, his voice sounded remote—as if he were discussing puppets in a play rather than us. "But then maybe the demons have seen to it that my kind of Revolution is out of date now."

I looked at Father in alarm. "What do you mean?"

Father shut his eyes and wrinkled his forehead with the same look of deep concentration that he wore when he fought with someone—but this time the opponent was himself. He stood there for a long time, and the only sound was the rain drumming heavily on the roof. "Maybe that's the truth that I've been trying to hide from myself. Maybe that's why I didn't want to recognize Foxfire as my son." He opened his eyelids abruptly. "I'm just a relic, and so are my ideas."

It took me a moment to find my voice. "You're not giving up on the Work, are you?"

He stared at me in a distant, abstracted way that made me feel as if I were a gem being studied by a jeweler for flaws. "No, I'm too old to change my habits. But I'm beginning to suspect that it's a time for the Foxfires and Cassias of this world."

I turned back to the stove, but as hot as the fire was, it didn't take away the strange chill that Father's words gave me. "You're scaring me with that kind of talk."

Father twisted me around so I would have to face him again. "It's an age for new dreams and for people who aren't afraid to make those dreams come true." And then he pressed his lips together in a thin smile. "It's an age for serpent children."

I wrapped an arm around Father. "Or maybe it's old seed growing in new earth."

Father shook his head slowly. "I still don't think I'll recognize the crop."

I huddled closer to him. "I just want us to be a family again."

Father looked down at me again. "Well, we are now—even if it's over such long distances." He added gently, "And that's all your mother could have asked of you."

Feeling warmer, I had to say one last time, "I wonder what Mother would say now."

Father tapped me on the nose. "Well, after any argument with me, she always dusted off her hands and said, 'So let's make the best of it anyway.' And then she'd brew us some tea."

I rubbed my nose as I looked at the shelves for the tea. "Then I will too," I promised.

Afterword

When I first began to research this story, my original intention was to discover my identity as a Chinese. However, like someone examining a family portrait, the closer I got, the more the faces seemed to dissolve into a collection of discrete dots. As a people, the Chinese were not the homogeneous whole that I had expected. The more I read, the more they seemed to divide into groups and subgroups. Moreover, the people from Kwangtung province, where this story takes place, did not fit at all into passive, self-effacing stereotypes.

I found the story of dreams and shadows during my high school days, and it has stayed with me to this time. It is actually a Greek tale, but I have heard a Chinese version. At any rate, the spirit of the tale has an Asian flavor and so I've used it. I have lost the notation on the original source, but I remember quite well reading the story in a book of the Loeb classical series.

Thanks are due to Michael Broschat who, without blinking an eyelid, tried to meet outrageous requests for various Chinese sources. I also wish to thank my agent, Pat Berens, who encouraged me to keep trying.

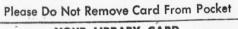